CAN'T RESIST
A COWBOY
PAINT RIVER RANCH

CAN'T RESIST A COWBOY

PAINT RIVER RANCH

ELIZABETH OTTO

Entangled Publishing
644 Shrewsbury Commons Ave
STE 181
Shrewsbury, PA 17361
rights@entangledpublishing.com

Indulgence is an imprint of Entangled Publishing.

Edited by Liz Pelletier
Cover design by Liz Pelletier
Cover photography from iStock

Manufactured in the United States of America

First Edition May 2015

Chapter One

A man dancing on the roof of the Tit for Tap bar with a squawking chicken under each arm should have been a little odd, but it was exactly the type of thing Carrie Lynn Waite expected around here. Surrounded by people, she crossed her arms and tipped her chin up to better see the show. The man started a little jig, somehow managing not to fall when the chickens went into freak-out mode. The crowd gave a raucous cheer and one corner of Carrie's mouth tugged up.

"What's this?" She slid her father, Darren, an amused look, indicating the roof.

He shrugged. "Supposed to be good luck."

She snorted. "For who?"

"Not the chickens." Darren winked and it did Carrie's heart good. Concern had overridden her happiness at being back in Montana when she'd arrived at her childhood home and found worsening disrepair. Agate Falls ranch had always needed a touch-up here or there, but this was different. Much, much worse. Once the centerpiece of the house, the wraparound porch was missing sections of railing. Steps were broken, the bottom one gone completely. And the crack in the living room window? She didn't have time to contemplate how that might have happened before her father led her to his truck and ushered her to the bar.

He'd tried to hide the creases in his forehead by pulling his cowboy hat low. It didn't fool her. She'd been his pillar for years. She'd become adept at sensing when shit was hitting the fan and he was trying to keep it to himself.

The man yelled something from above and stumbled. Carrie caught her breath. One chicken went flying, making an arc through the fading daylight, wings flapping to beat hell as it plummeted into the waiting hands of the crowd.

The roof dancer raised his free arm over his head and bellowed, "May Fire!" and the crowd cheered, holding plastic beer cups high. Slow warmth filled her chest at the pronouncement. May Fire, the start of cattle branding season in Greenbrook, Montana, was something she'd missed since moving away five years ago. It was a celebration of community and a time for the local ranchers to get together for food, drinks, and the bonfire that gave the event its name.

Carrie tilted her head to adjust for the dimming sunlight, momentarily closing her eyes against the glare. A shout from up top startled her into looking. The second bird made a descent, falling straight at her. Carrie stepped forward, her arms going out instinctively to make a cradle for the poor thing as it landed with an ear-piercing squawk.

Shocked, Carrie breathed a sigh of relief, the chicken's heart racing as it settled into her embrace and promptly tucked its head into the crook of her arm. Darren shook his head and tipped his hat back.

"You always did have the touch, Carrie-girl. You could put the meanest dog to sleep with a little scratch." It was true. She had the gift of touch—at least that's what he'd always said. Her job in Wyoming as a massage therapist played to her skills, and she was good at it. There was nothing quite like the satisfaction of taking someone's stress and pain away.

Mindlessly stroking the chicken, Carrie looked around for a place to deposit the bird as she followed her dad inside the Tit for Tap. They hadn't gotten far when he stopped and turned to her.

"Welcome home, honey. I didn't get a chance to tell you earlier."

"Thanks, Dad." His request for her to visit couldn't have come at a better time. She'd been planning to take a long vacation at Agate Falls anyway. Five months had passed since she'd last been home, and she needed a quiet place to do some heavy thinking. She couldn't shake the impression she'd have more to think about soon, given the state of the ranch.

He studied her a moment. "We need to sit down and have a good talk." Their weekly phone conversations hadn't tipped her off to any bad news brewing, but her dad had always been good at keeping things to himself until he just couldn't hold it in any longer.

"By the way…" His expression grew serious. "Just 'cause you're home at branding time doesn't mean you're working. You just sit back and watch."

A diabetic since childhood, she'd struggled with hard-to-regulate blood sugar levels starting around puberty. The physical labors of ranching life seemed to make it worse. A few hours of horseback riding or working the fields and her sugars would plummet and she'd faint, sometimes suffering injuries as a result. After she'd passed out in the barn and broken her arm, her doctors suggested a radical lifestyle change to try to help.

No ranch work. No horseback riding. No extreme physical labor. Agate Falls was an hour from the closest hospital, and it had been stressful on her father to constantly worry about her. By the time she was thirteen, she'd been homeschooled with a tutor and placed on an activity restriction. She'd spent the bulk of her younger years on the sidelines, watching while ranching went on around her, resenting every moment she couldn't participate.

Eventually, her body adjusted and she had less trouble regulating her sugar. When she'd turned eighteen, her dad had urged her to move to the city to live with her aunts where medical care was easily available. She'd left, gone to college, and gotten a job as a chiropractic assistant and massage therapist. But she'd missed Agate Falls every day since.

A stream of people had formed behind her, urging them forward. Carrie was nearly pushed into her dad's back as they shuffled inside. "So, where is branding tomorrow?"

The glance he cast over his shoulder spoke for him. She groaned. There were five ranches in Greenbrook; why did it have to be *that* one?

"Paint River Ranch." Just saying the words gave her a shot of longing and the shadowy memory of turquoise eyes looking down into hers. Her scalp tingled as she struggled with the sudden need to turn around and search the sea of faces. Damn it, she already had—the moment she'd stepped out of the truck in the bar's parking lot. There'd been no sign of the Haywood boys, Cole, Tucker, and Levi, anywhere. Good. She'd run into *him* eventually, she supposed. *Eventually* could hold out a little longer.

Tightening her grip on the chicken, Carrie stepped over the threshold of the bar and handed the bird to the bouncer. He leaned back on his stool with both palms in the air. "No way. Deep fryer's in the back."

She mirrored his playful grin. "Seriously?" Tempted to launch the bird and make a run for it, Carrie followed her dad inside. The dim interior light made her squint.

Darren spoke into her ear like he had a secret. "Levi's going to be here tonight. Been a good few years since you seen him, huh?"

Well, *eventually* just got a whole lot shorter. A good few years since she'd seen him? That had been on purpose. The bastard had ditched her six years ago and never looked back, and no matter how much she'd missed him all this time, her pride kept the longing in check.

"He's all healed up," her dad continued as if this were an ordinary topic and not one that hurt. Time had passed; he probably figured she was over it. Mostly, she was, though there were still moments when she lost herself in what she'd had with Levi, and what could have been—if he hadn't dumped her.

Carrie's arm tensed around the bird, one hand stroking him to keep her nerves under control. The Haywoods were their neighbors. Growing up, their families had helped each other with ranch work, and spent a fair amount of free time together. Levi had been her friend before he'd been her first love—and the first to crush her soul into a gazillion pieces.

Thanks to his brother Tucker keeping her in the loop over the years, she knew Levi had almost lost his life in Afghanistan and was subsequently healed. Her connection to the Haywoods ran deep. Though it had pained her heart each time Tucker texted or called with a tidbit, it agonized her more to consider asking him to stop updating her. She and Levi had too much history, she supposed, to ever be completely erased from each other's lives.

"Geez, girl. You're going to pet the feathers clean off him."

"What?" She looked down, realizing she was petting the bird too hard. She wished her diabetes didn't keep her from drinking, because something strong sounded perfect right about now.

"You okay?"

Carrie feigned indifference. She'd let go of Levi a long time ago, and it was going to stay that way. When she saw him again, she'd hold in six long years of emotion and be polite and composed. She'd say hello and get it over fast, like ripping off a Band-Aid, before her brain and heart had the chance to get stupid over him.

Luckily, her dad didn't pry anymore. "I'm going to mingle a bit on the way to the bar. Get us a table?" Darren left to flag down a waitress. A band geared up to play from the stage, the crowd getting louder and rowdier by the second. Aware that she was still in the path of people coming in the door, Carrie moved to the side and looked for a place to sit as the shadows continued to mess with her depth perception.

A huge *bang* from the back of the dance floor made her jump. A collective gasp of surprise went through the space. Light filtered in the far end of the room as if the back door had been opened and the crowd made a dash to part down the middle. Someone shouted, "Damn it, Cody, not again!" as a huge shadow shot down the path the crowd had made.

"Horse in the bar!" was followed by a cheer that seemed amazingly out of place, because, really? A horse? Though she did have a chicken… It took Carrie's brain a moment to register. Yep, horse, trotting through the room with its rider whooping, "May Fire!" and waving his hat in the air. She searched for an escape, but the distorted shadows left her no clear path to follow.

The horse's hooves sounded like hollow thunder on the wood floor—getting louder as it headed straight for her. A man burst off his chair next to her, inadvertently knocking it in her direction as she tried to sidestep out of the horse's path. Carrie tripped, right arm going out to help her balance, left arm squeezing the bird. She wobbled the wrong way, stumbling forward instead of back as the planks vibrated under her feet.

A cry lodged in her throat as a puff of warm horse breath washed over her face, the animal so close, she could feel its body heat.

Carrie tensed, preparing for impact.

Chapter Two

"I'm a dude, and this is against every single man code ever made."

"You owe me, little brother. It's time to pay up."

Levi Haywood finished off the Coke in his plastic cup and moved away from the heat of the bonfire. He couldn't believe he was having this conversation with his middle brother, Tucker, out here in the open field behind the bar where anyone could overhear the ridiculousness of it. Fine, he owed his brother a hand to make up for all the years Levi had been away. Helping their mother set up a spa on the ranch? Damn insulting.

Ignoring a twinge of pain in his leg, he leaned closer to Tucker and kept his voice low. "Fine. But let it be noted that as a marine *and* a man, I'm not happy about it." Facials, creams, scented oils, and all that waxing was a woman's forte—though he did love the feel of a smooth, bare, freshly waxed pu… *No.* No way. Levi crossed his arms. He had limits, even where the holy grail of waxed lady bits was concerned.

Tucker flicked the toothpick in his mouth with a cocky

smile. "Yeah, well let it be noted that I don't give a shit how you feel about it."

Levi crumpled the cup in his palm. The past three months or so, he'd been healed up and strong enough to work hard. After nearly having his legs blown off in Afghanistan, he'd gone through months in bed and endless hours of physical therapy to get this far. He even shocked himself sometimes with how well he'd bounced back.

Good old Haywood spirit, his brothers said. Levi figured that might be part of it, but mostly, no good man could handle lying around on his ass that long. Not when each sunrise offered him the opportunity to get his feet back on Paint River soil. Problem was, the ranch's tourist and cattle operations had grown considerably while he'd been in the marines. They had a full staff now, and not a lot for Levi but odds and ends. His oldest brother, Cole, was in charge of almost everything, with the overflow falling to Tucker and their lead ranch hand, Jaxon. That left little for Levi to do—and even if there had been, there was no way in hell the mess of them could try to work at anything together. Not without a lot of cussing and spilled blood.

So he'd found something for himself to do, something that was going to keep him very busy.

"Just think," Tucker went on when Levi didn't respond, "a spa attracts women. Consider it a mission to help the single men of Paint River Ranch get laid. Which includes you. All you have to do is sit in on the business interviews with Ma and help her figure out how much space a spa is going to take up. Easy."

Yeah, easy. He looked to the horizon and made a disgruntled sound. Fading daylight punched the sky with orange and red. The mountain range took his angst away— just brushed it right out of him. Cool May air filled his lungs, and he savored it. Clean, crisp, not a hint of dust or sand to burn his throat and chest.

He hadn't found a good time to tell his family about his project. It was a big one that didn't involve playing metrosexual. The opportunity had been too personal to pass up. Considering his constant boredom, it couldn't have come at a better time.

"Yeah, all right." The tension in his shoulders faded. He'd help his family out with the spa. Didn't mean he had to like it. Seemed he'd be going from zero to sixty here real soon. Good. Bring it. He was ready.

A voice he recognized cut through the crowd. He looked as Darren Waite, the owner of Agate Falls ranch, and their neighbor, socialized his way around. He paused as the older man caught his gaze. They exchanged a nod, and for a second, Levi thought he might come over, but the rancher continued on. Levi had the sudden memory of warm brown eyes and lush pink lips smiling up at him. At one time, where Darren went, so did his sweet blond-haired daughter, Carrie Lynn.

Seemed like a lifetime ago that they'd grown up side by side, always together. It had been effortless, natural, the way they'd grown to love each other… and crushing the way he had ended it. Levi winced internally. The last time he'd seen Carrie, he'd been a boy in a man's body—directionless and full of wanderlust. He'd wanted off the ranch to experience life outside Montana's borders, and he'd made the choice knowing that he'd lose her. He hoped someday he'd forgive himself for ripping them apart—that maybe one day he'd be able to explain to her why he'd done it—but neither had come to pass.

He'd held the gift of their shared time close to his heart all these years, letting the memories sustain him through two tours in Afghanistan and all the days and nights in between. Though he hadn't seen her in years, he had heard from his brothers that she lived in Wyoming with her aunts and was still single—a tidbit they liked to toss in whenever her name came up.

The memory seemed to drive his pain, giving him a sharp pinch and dull ache in one punch. Levi let out a hard breath. Residual discomfort was a byproduct of leg muscles that didn't work the same anymore. Sometimes, it escalated and ripped through him, refusing to die until he downed a couple pain pills. He never knew when it might get that bad.

"I'm ready to get out of here." Levi turned toward the bar and walked inside, the touch of his dog tags hard and cool against his chest beneath his T-shirt.

"Arm wrestle you for it," Tucker called out as he caught up. "I win, we stay. You win, we go."

Levi paused for the crowd to clear so he could get through. "Dude, your biceps are illegal in ten states. Wouldn't be fair." Teasing his brother gave him a bit of much-needed lightness inside until a shout drew him out of his thoughts. The noise turned into a roar that rolled through the bar. People around him scattered, giving Levi a clear view.

A *very* clear view of a horse trotting through the bar. A chair skidded across the floor right at a woman who tried to avoid it. But her foot caught the chair and she stumbled straight into the path of the horse. Realizing he was close enough to reach her, Levi lurched forward and grabbed the back of her denim jacket. Pain shot through his leg as he tried to pull her back. She tumbled backward at an angle and landed in the crook of his arm as the horse raced past them and out the front door. His eyes locked with the woman's and all the swear words in his head hit a wall and splattered into one blinding thought: *Carrie*.

The rise and fall of her denim jacket stopped about the same time he forgot how to do that air-in and air-out thing. His sunshine. Here.

"Carrie Lynn."

He blinked hard and she mirrored the action. The noise around them was real, the chatter of voices, close. Still, he wasn't sure if he'd slipped into a dream, or if this was really happening. The last time he'd seen Carrie, he'd been looking down into her huge brown eyes just like this. Only then her expression had been filled with sated passion…not the rampant blend of confusion and shock that flickered over her face right now.

And she hadn't been holding a chicken.

"Levi." Her voice was a breathy whisper, filled with the same longing that had quietly pulsed in his heart every day for the past six years. Guiding her up, Levi flexed his fingers against her back, positive he was going to blink and she'd be gone. The touch grounded him, and as he slowly looked her over, it became apparent that she was very, very real.

Curly blond hair escaped her ponytail, the smell of sweet shampoo swirling in the space between them. A denim jacket covered most of the lacy green dress that she wore. Brown boots came up to her knees, allowing only a narrow strip of skin to show between the tops and the hem of her dress. Her softly rounded cheekbones and square chin with the tiny dimple in the middle were the same he'd dreamed about endlessly. Soft, warm…she smelled amazing in that beguiling, irresistible way he'd always loved about her.

Her brow furrowed as an urgent little sound escaped her full pink lips. "I have a chicken."

He smiled, too stunned to do anything else. Carrie's free hand came up, and she paused before tucking a stray hair behind her ear. Slowly, she brought her hand to his face, fingertips grazing his jaw, and he found himself leaning into her touch. The touch was quick and warm, robbing his breath and squeezing his heart. Goddamn, how could his brain be swimming yet calm at the same time?

He lightly gripped her wrist, wanting to cover her hand with his, but she pulled away. Afraid he'd moved too fast or something, he took a small step back to give them space. Not that he wanted space. In the span of a few minutes he'd gone from missing her to having her fall into his arms. Now that the shock had let go, he was perfectly aware that the woman he'd never stopped loving was *here*.

And she looked like she might be sick. Nearly getting run over by a horse had shocked the hell out of her. Or...was it him?

Needing contact, he lightly touched her arm. "Are you okay?"

She nodded quickly. "I'm fine... I have to put her outside." She turned to leave.

No, not yet!

"Carrie, wait." Her shoulders tensed and he thought she would turn back, but she didn't.

She walked, the crowd swallowing her whole. Levi clenched his jaw and forced himself not to follow her. This wasn't how he'd imagined seeing her again to go. It wasn't enough; he needed more time. This nanosecond meeting had been just two paths crossing and damn it, he wanted a reunion.

Chapter Three

Ribbons of pink, orange, and silver rose behind grayed mountain peaks. Carrie shoved her gloved hands into the pockets of her canvas coat. Morning wind laced through her hair and chilled her face. Invigorated, her mind seemed clear, her body pumping with energy. It was so good to be out of the city and in the middle of nothing but the natural beauty that had always sustained her.

She was on Paint River Ranch land, but the view was virtually the same as from Agate Falls—scenery she soaked up and tucked away. No matter how many times she'd seen the sunrise as a kid, it never got old. It was one of those beautiful things so easy to take for granted, thinking you'll see it again. Until the time comes when you don't.

When you can't.

Noise came in muted bursts behind her. Cattle bellowing. Metal gates clanking closed. Men hollering back and forth. Her dad had gotten her up at four thirty this morning and shoved a cup of coffee in her hand with the question she'd been dreading. "You coming with?"

She'd wanted to refuse. After the Levi fiasco last night, she didn't have the heart to run into him again. *I have a chicken.* What the hell had she been thinking? After all this time, *that* was the best line she could come up with? She blushed just thinking about it. That facing him was uncomfortable and awkward was, well, expected.

Skipping branding today was her ticket out of seeing him again so soon, but she'd missed so much over the years. Time was slowly, insidiously ticking down for her, and one day she wouldn't experience this place and all its activity in the same way. She needed to see it all, to soak it up and hang on to it.

She'd never been the sentimental type, but figured going blind did that to a person.

"Carrie!" She turned to see her father waving her over. With a last look to the sky, she strolled down to the cattle pens. Her dad walked off before she reached him, but she didn't mind. Most of her night had been spent pulled to pieces over how to break the news to him that she was losing her eyesight. He'd be devastated, probably more than she'd been at hearing the news for the first time. Though she'd known for a while, Carrie had tucked it away, waiting for the right time. When he'd called and asked her to come home for a visit, she figured it was now or never. Never was still more appealing.

Stopping to lean against the tailgate of a truck by the pen, she glanced around. There were many faces she didn't know—Paint River Ranch had grown over the years by expanding into a tourist and recreation location. Rows of pretty red-and-white cabins, a new store and office building, and an area for an in-ground swimming pool met her as they'd pulled in this morning. It seemed every time she visited, the ranch had sacrificed more good land to expand its guest accommodations.

Cattle ranching was a tough, uncertain business, often necessitating other ways to make money when beef prices were low. A few other area ranches had followed in the Haywoods' footsteps by inviting in tourists. The rest, like Agate Falls, had clung tightly to their cattle-rearing roots. It was hard to see Paint River grow so commercially, but she understood why the Haywoods did it. Survival.

Pouring a cup of coffee from a thermos on the tailgate, Carrie looked into the dark brew with a nostalgic pang. Her granddaddy's image came to mind. With a never-empty tin mug of mud-dark coffee clutched in one hand, he'd tuck an unlit cigarette behind his ear, his other arm around her shoulders as they watched the sun come up behind Agate Falls' barn. He'd say, "This is ranching land. As far as your eye can see." And pat her on the head, as if the simple gesture could cement that statement forever.

"Carrie Lynn!" She looked up for the source of the feminine voice, but Cole and Tucker Haywood rode past on their horses, blocking her view. She gave a short wave, both men calling out a greeting as they rode past, leaving her wondering where Levi was. She didn't have time to worry about it when she spotted Maeve Haywood, Cole, Tucker, and Levi's mother, waving at her. She made her way over and was immediately wrapped in Maeve's embrace.

"It's been a long time!" Like a surrogate mother, Maeve had always been there with a loving smile or a warm hug, enveloping Carrie into her family. There'd been a time it had seemed a given that she really would become part of this family, back when she and Levi were inseparable.

"It's good to see you, Maeve." More than she dared express, actually. Her emotions were getting soppy and messy, drumming up potent homesickness. Why was all this nonsense rushing her now? She'd been home for a few days five months ago and though sad to leave, she hadn't experienced this raw, unearthed longing. She hadn't visited Paint River then. Maybe it was a combination of both places this time.

Clearing her throat, she willed the emotional spigot to turn off. Maeve hooked her arm through Carrie's, and turned them toward two women she hadn't noticed before. "Let me introduce my daughters-in-law—Rylan, Cole's wife. And Sophie, who's stuck with Tucker."

"You've got that right," Sophie quipped with an affectionate grin. Rylan ran a hand over her very pregnant belly and gave a disgruntled groan.

"I can't believe he got me up so early for this," Rylan grumbled.

Sophie nudged her on the arm. "You should have the baby today, *right now*, just on principle." She patted a red medical-looking kit with a silvery Star of Life on the top slung over her shoulder and leaned to Rylan's belly. "I'm ready, honey. Any time now."

With a laugh, Rylan pushed her sister-in-law away and shook her head. "Sophie's a paramedic part time in Missoula. Thinks she's going to deliver my baby here at the ranch. *No way*." The two women had a good-natured stare-down before Rylan leaned on Sophie with a sigh and closed her eyes. "I'm glad you're here, Soph. Just in case."

Carrie smiled though something akin to jealousy went through her. She had friends in Wyoming, and her aunts, but her family was mostly reduced to her and her dad. What would it be like, to be part of a family this big and close?

Maeve waved off her daughters-in-law. "You look good, Carrie. Real good."

"She sure does."

A shiver went down her spine at the familiar timbre. She didn't have to turn to know it was Levi. Her body remembered. She glanced back as he walked by leading a horse and holding leather gloves in one hand. Despite the chill, he was only clad in a black thermal top and jeans. No hat to cover the glossy mess of wavy black hair. No chaps to hide the long lines of his legs. The blue of his eyes made her breath catch as he locked onto her, gave a nod, and kept on going.

It was surreal, seeing him walk past like so many memories of him had sauntered through her mind. He stopped at the corral gate and glanced back at her with a cocky, half-tilted smile. Six years flew away like chaff on the wind, leaving behind the rightness of him and her in this moment, the way they had been so many times before. He'd rope the cattle. She'd keep the branding irons hot in the fire. They'd share smiles and secret grins, and rib each other the entire day. Until night came and they could slip away...

"Carrie? Help me get more coffee and breakfast set out?"

"Yes." She jerked back to Maeve, her mind pulled between the past and the present. If the soft smile on the older woman's face was any indication, she knew what Carrie had been thinking. But this wasn't the past. It was now, and her future wasn't bright. Levi might be healed up and finding his rhythm back home on the ranch, but she was off balance and nowhere near ready to deal with a cowboy who'd broken her heart.

She had two weeks here to spend with her dad and enjoy being home. The less she saw of Levi to mess with that, the better.

The morning passed in a blur of bellowing cattle and the scent of flesh heated under molten steel. In between light tasks and helping Maeve set out lunch, Carrie found herself peeking at Levi here and there. It wasn't long before she was totally engrossed in watching as he guided his horse to cut cattle from the herd and sent them toward Cole and Tucker to be roped and lowered to the ground. After a while, he and Cole switched duties and Levi handled the roped cattle with an admirable stride.

In between being serious and focused, he would joke with his brothers and flash that wicked smile. Each time she tried to pull herself away, he'd look her way and she'd be inclined to watch just a little longer. The lines of his body, his face, were so familiar but different. He'd aged, of course, but with a subtle hardness that most twenty-six-year-old men didn't have. Who could blame him for having a rough edge after what he'd gone through?

Going to war and being injured would break a lot of men. Maybe it had broken him, at least a little. Every now and then, his jaw would clench, his brow furrowing as if he were in pain. It came and went, making her wonder if it was discomfort or something else. Whatever it was, he pushed it behind a smile or his serious face and got back to work.

The men finally came over for lunch, mainlining coffee like it was lifesaving elixir and shoveling chili down their throats. Feeling to make sure the packet containing her insulin was in her pocket, Carrie ate some crackers as she wandered to her father by the fence. He was talking to a man whose name she couldn't recall. Their backs were to her, their voices low but solid enough that she could hear.

"…real happy you were able to stop the auction, Darren. You know Susie and I were prepared to help however we could."

"Thanks, Bill. Appreciate that."

"It'd have been a shame to see your place pieced apart." With that, he slapped Darren on the arm, looking up and giving her a nod.

Carrie froze. Auction…pieced apart? Her dad spun, his face falling as he spotted her. The other man walked off and a couple seconds passed before her lips stopped tingling enough to speak. "What was that about?"

He shrugged her off and dug into his chili. "Thought we could talk about it later, Carrie."

"Auction?" She crossed her arms, her own lunch forgotten. "What auction?" Her mind began to run through the possibilities. *Please don't say Agate Falls… Please don't…*

"Agate Falls."

Her chin snapped up. Things had been going to shit

around the ranch. That wasn't a secret. But he'd always promised to fix it—forever had an excuse and a way of putting it off. He was normally slow about getting to things, so she hadn't overly worried.

"God, Dad. Why...what happened?"

He set his bowl on the ground and tipped back his hat. "Beef prices fell and our hay's been bad the past couple of years. I couldn't catch up. For the first time, I couldn't float by until it got better." He looked past her, up to the sky. "I didn't want to tell you over the phone. Didn't want you to worry."

She gripped the fence rail, the metal cool under her hand. For years, the focus had been on her health and moving her to the city. Once she'd gone, she'd become oblivious to the day-to-day at the ranch. God, she should have visited more, paid more attention and realized that things really *were* falling apart and not just in the queue to be attended to.

Throat tight, Carrie embraced him, hoping her arms would tell him what her voice couldn't. He patted her back, the stubble on his jaw rough against her cheek.

"It's okay, Carrie. I, uh, took on an investor. He has good plans to pull us through."

She pulled back. He'd had the opportunity to partner with investors before and would never consider it. Holding on to his land was like gripping his pride. They'd all heard stories of slimy investors waiting like vultures to swoop down and feed on vulnerable ranches, or golden-tongued developers throwing money and sweet talk around. She gripped his wrist, hoping like hell he hadn't taken up with either type.

"Who?"

Footsteps crunched in the dirt behind her. Her dad looked over her shoulder, and curious, she turned to look. Levi stopped and pulled his gloves off, finger by finger, his lips a serious line.

"Me."

Chapter Four

Levi was going to have to quit for the day if the pain in his legs got any worse, and that just plain pissed him off. The left was always the worst, having taken the bulk of the bomb hit all those months ago. What thigh muscle the doctors had been able to save was testy about working too hard. He was supposed to limit strenuous physical activity to short sessions. Being on a horse and roping cattle for five hours straight was too long, apparently.

Because damn.

Unintentionally walking up on Darren and Carrie's conversation gave him something else to focus on besides his discomfort. He hadn't meant to eavesdrop, but he couldn't just pass on by after overhearing them. Plus, Darren had spotted him, his shoulders relaxing a bit as if relieved Levi had shown up when he did.

He couldn't read Carrie's expression, and he didn't mind studying her a while longer to figure it out. Dreams hadn't done her beauty justice.

"You?" She pointed a finger at him, the narrow set of her

eyes reminding him how fast her temper could be. "You're kidding, right?"

The admonishment in her voice was a kick in the pride. What did he expect? She wasn't going to fall all over him in gratitude—she was right to be wary. He couldn't deny that, in part, he'd done this for her. He wasn't going to stand by as the ranch get sold off, not with all the love and memories wrapped up in that place. Agate Falls and Paint River had shared help, land, and resources for as long as Levi could remember. When he'd found out the ranch was one push away from going to auction, he'd jumped at the chance to help.

"We're neighbors. It just made sense."

"What are you going to do with our land?" She looked to her father, but he didn't look back. His eyes were locked on Levi.

"Carrie," Darren said softly. "I couldn't let Agate Falls go like that. Honey, it's going to be yours someday—I couldn't lose the ranch knowing I'd robbed you of that. This is a good thing."

Her eyes clenched tight right before she rubbed them with a thumb. "No, Dad. It's not going to be mi..." With a sigh, she pulled a pair of sunglasses from her pocket and put them on. "I have to do my insulin." Shoving her hands in her pockets, Carried turned toward the house and walked away.

"I should have told her sooner." Darren picked up his bowl off the ground. "It wasn't right of me to leave her in the dark." Levi could only nod as the older man wandered away. He was right; he should have told Carrie sooner. He understood trying to find the right time and all to talk about something like this. Hell, he still hadn't told his brothers about his involvement in Agate Falls. It wasn't his business to get mixed up in what happened between Carrie and her dad, so why did he feel guilty? He looked to the sky, knowing full well why. She'd had people making decisions that involved her, without her input, for years. Including him.

A deep ache went through his left thigh, reminding him he was overdue for some pain reliever before he got back on his horse. Waving down his friend and ranch hand, Jaxon Moore, Levi nodded to his horse tied at the gate. "Cover me for a few." Jax gave a thumbs-up, and Levi headed to the house. He'd catch Carrie—smooth things over for now until they could get a better chance to talk.

He went up the back steps; it felt like a wolf was gnawing on his leg. Grabbing pain pills from the kitchen cabinet, he made it to the couch before his knee buckled and a twisted cramp rippled through his thigh.

"Son of a bitch," he hissed, gritting his teeth against the spasm as he sat. A cool line of sweat beaded along his hairline. *Pain is honor. Pain is honor.* The words rolled like a chant in his head, a familiar pattern he'd learned in boot camp, where physical pain and mental fatigue were an everyday thing. It had been a while since it had been this bad, but it would pass. It would.

He'd been working too hard, but damn it, he'd had enough of being idle. Now he was paying for it.

"Levi?" A warm touch on his shoulder followed his name. Vanilla, something spicy and girlie, met him as he glanced up. Carrie looked down at him, the smooth lines of her face heavy with worry. Her eyes were so big, so brown. Lashes went on forever.

"Charley horse?" She dropped to her knees beside him and placed a hand on the top of his knotted leg.

A flicker of panic went through him. It was bad enough that she was seeing him like this. He didn't want her finding out how damaged his body was, too. "I just need to walk it out." Ha. Right. He couldn't get up right now if his ass was on fire. "I'm fine."

"No, you're not." Carrie smoothed her palm over his

jeans, the pressure and friction both painful and soothing. "I can help." Help—with her hands on him? Despite the thickness of his jeans, she'd be able to feel the mangled mess of his leg beneath. There was no shame in the scars, but he wasn't ready for her reaction. He didn't want to see pity, or worse, disgust on her face.

"Don't." The request was weak, but his pride was strong. Levi leaned forward to get up. Enough of this. He'd walk it out and get back to work.

"Relax, Levi." Her hands were already working over his jeans, pressing her fingers into the space above the knee where muscle met bone. Tingles raced up like an electrical circuit to his groin, a forceful breath rushing out of him. She held her fingers there, pressing deeply.

And then her palms moved over his middle thigh, her fingers massaging and kneading, pulling and smoothing until he was captured in a blend of discomfort and relief. Her movements weren't gentle, but they were helping. The pain began to fade…his body relaxed and his chest expanded so he could breathe. Her touch softened a bit as she worked her magic down past his knee, to his calf and back up again.

He'd had therapeutic massages on his legs before, but he'd never felt so fluid afterward. By the time she sat back on her heels, Levi's leg was singing hymns and angels were flying around the room.

"Holy shit." He gripped a fistful of his hair. "That was amazing."

She laughed. "Ah, you're welcome." He fully realized that she was on her knees next to him. Her hair had come free of the ponytail and lay draped in a haphazard curls over her shoulders.

"Thank you," he blurted. A new kind of ache started in his body, the kind that got stronger when he looked at her full lips and wondered if they still tasted as sweet as he remembered. She shifted as if to get up, her shoulder brushing against his knee. The simple contact jacked his longing for one kiss…just one. Levi reached for her, moving so his legs were on either side of her as he pulled her up halfway and wrapped his arms around her.

He tensed as her full, soft breasts pushed against his chest, her breath warm and humid against the curve of his throat. She uttered something akin to a sob as her arms wound around his neck. He wanted to bury his face in her hair, hold her tighter, trail his lips over her skin…but he had no right. What was he doing? He should back away, but her fingers were wrapped around him tightly, giving the impression she wanted to stay just like this.

God, he'd missed her. If her embrace was an indication, she'd missed him, too.

With a start, Carrie released him and fumbled to stand. She tucked her hair behind her ears. Levi rose, amazed at how steady he was considering how badly he'd been feeling minutes earlier. She wouldn't look at him, and the sudden awkwardness reminded him that they were strangers. Maybe they'd stay that way, maybe they'd come to reconnect some. Either way, they needed to find some common ground—a way to get on during the duration of her stay. He'd be around Agate Falls a lot in the coming days, and the last thing he wanted was to make her uncomfortable.

Thinking of it, he realized he had no idea how long she'd be in Montana.

"I'm glad it helped." The sound of her voice was startling in the quiet room.

"Yeah." He figured he should apologize for the embrace, but he wasn't a lick sorry about it. Touching her was as close to heaven as he'd experienced in a while. That was something, considering he'd been on the very short list for a personal tour once already.

Reaching behind her head, she gathered her hair into a fresh ponytail, nailing him with a conflicted look. A chill seemed to replace the heat they'd just shared. That was his cue to get back to work and leave this on a somewhat positive note. Moving to a small side table by the couch, he grabbed a bottle of pain reliever he'd left there earlier.

"Levi." Her hard tone made him pause. "Promise me you'll do right by my father."

He opened the bottle, trying to ignore the frustration creeping up. "We have a lot to talk about, Carrie. Once we—"

Her arms crossed. "Promise me."

He poured two pills into his palm, swallowed them dry. The insult in her request was quiet, but it was there. She didn't trust him, and he didn't blame her. He'd love nothing more than to hash out their past and work for that common ground, but he had cattle to get back to. Shoving the bottle in his pocket, Levi walked past her toward the door. "What makes you think I won't?"

She cut in front, looking over her shoulder at him before pushing the door open and walking out. "History."

Chapter Five

Hands on her hips, Carrie glanced around the attic with a small sense of defeat. The space used to be neatly organized but was now crammed with so much stuff she had no idea where to find what she wanted. The disarray wasn't just confined to this room, unfortunately. She'd taken a good, long look around the ranch and the house this morning. With her dad gone running errands, she'd been free to examine the place without worrying about hurting his feelings. He'd tried to keep the ranch tip-top, but truthfully it was a disaster.

Broken gate panels, cracked windows in the barns, and clogged water pipes were just a few things she'd noticed. Add the disrepairs on the ranch house and it all equaled one huge project. A man with as much pride as her father would keep going as long as possible, and strive to fix whatever he could. But it had snowballed, the repairs coming faster than cash flow until it all piled up and he crouched under the weight of it all.

Enter Levi, with his piles of Paint River money and hot muscles to save the day. She made a disgusted sound and began shuffling boxes around. He'd done a good thing, helping them out. He wasn't just military. He'd been a hardworking cowboy before that. Honor and all that were ingrained in him. The ranchers helped each other around here. It's just how things were done. But his money had secured him a place at Agate Falls, one with decision-making ability. What if he decided to bend the ranch into a tourist hot spot, like Paint River?

The thought made her nearly drop a box.

Is that what had her so on edge? It would be a cop-out to admit that was the only reason. It was his very presence back in her life. They shared a past, one that hadn't been resolved very well. He'd waited until the night before he left for boot camp to tell her he'd even signed up for the marines. When tear-filled hours had brought the daylight, he'd been gone, and he'd stayed gone for six long years.

She'd daydreamed about reconnecting with him, but now that it was happening, she wasn't sure it was a good thing. The hug they'd shared yesterday had sent her into a tailspin of emotions. It had felt so good to be pressed against him again, to feel the silken edges of his hair curl around her fingers. To hear his voice, and feel the soft pump of his heart under her chest. But she was leaving in two measly weeks, back to the prison of the city where her health demanded she stay. She and Levi had a huge divide between them and not enough time to close it. Even if they did, what good would come of it?

She'd fall in love with him again and would be the one walking away this time.

She yanked the cover off a plastic tub. Nostalgia hit her when she spied old Christmas decorations inside. On the top lay a crocheted angel made stiff with a wash of salt water and glue, a little golden pipe-cleaner halo on her head. Maeve Haywood had given it to her the year Carrie's mother had died in a car accident.

Laying the angel in her palm, Carrie blew her bangs from

her eyes. She should have taken care to stay in touch with Maeve more after Levi left. Selfishness had kept her from it. The need to separate herself from memories of him had been stronger than her affection for the Haywoods. All of them had expected that she and Levi would be making a wedding announcement, joining the two ranches officially as one big happy family. They'd been just as shocked as she had been to learn that Levi was leaving.

"Jerk," she said out loud. Enough of thinking about Levi. She put the angel back and was just closing the box when she spotted a glint of yellow in the sunlight coming through the dormer window. With a squeal of joy, Carrie carefully moved away a stack of old papers. Behind it, a three-foot-tall rectangular window stood. The lighting was nearly perfect inside the attic. Not so dim that she could only see shadows, but not so bright as to blind her. Naked save for a fine layer of dust, the stained glass teased her with brilliant colors. She sighed happily and tipped the panel up. A beam of sunlight fractured off the sunflower pattern, casting myriad jewel tones.

Her breath caught. She'd dabbled in stained glass as a teen as a way to cure her boredom at being on "restricted activity" to help her diabetes. After Levi had left, she'd thrown herself into making this panel, cutting all the small, colorful pieces that created a large sunflower and ruby-red cardinals. The lead beading between each piece could have been smoother, the shapes, more carefully cut. But then it had been a way of healing and given her a huge sense of accomplishment.

Now it was a reminder that she still had her sight, and she needed to appreciate *everything* as often as possible. It could be years or it could be months, her doctor had said. With diabetic neuropathy, there was no telling how fast her sight would fade. The upside was that, for now, only her left eye was showing major decline. The right side could hold out longer, giving her hope that though her vision would be compromised, it would take a long time to fade completely. Keeping her blood sugar under control could help.

So back to the city it was, where her low-stress desk job and immediate access to health care were there to help her stay healthy.

Thinking that she'd take the panel back to Wyoming as a reminder of home, Carrie was distracted by the sound of vehicles outside. Laying aside the glass, she crossed to the other dormer and peeked out over the pasture that lined the road and eventually connected with Paint River land.

In the distance, the original cabin her great-grandfather had built when he'd settled the ranch sat in a clearing lined by a thin row of pines. Three white trucks and a backhoe rolled along the fence line until they stopped, a man jumping out of the first truck. Raising her hand to cut the glare, Carrie squinted, making out enough to see a man cut the wire fence, creating a large enough gap that the vehicles could get through.

Her dad hadn't said anything about work being done around here today. Something about the unmarked white trucks and their proximity to the cabin made her gut sink with dread. Going downstairs, Carrie got into her Chevy and drove down the road, slowing as the backhoe made a ramble through the makeshift gate. Cell phone in hand, ready to call her dad, she got out and approached the first man she saw. An embroidered logo on his shirt read "Zane Engineering & Surveying."

"What's going on?"

The man smiled with a mouthful of perfect teeth and extended a hand. "Ms....?"

"Waite. Darren Waite's daughter."

"Right." He put his hands on his hips, eyes crinkling like he was thrilled to be here. "We're getting started on the soil testing and land survey."

The hairs on the back of her neck prickled. To the left, the backhoe got awfully close to her granddaddy's cabin. "For what?"

The man gave her a curious look, and then swept his arm to indicate a wide circle around them. "For the campground."

...

"And this one is Choco-licious, our most popular."

Levi gave a polite smile to the blonde sitting across from him, though he didn't give a shit about the tube of goo she held. This was the third spa interview he'd had to sit through this morning, and he cared about Jennie's Delights exactly the same amount as he had Viva Day Spa and Evergreen Massage & More: zero. All of the women they'd met with so far seemed determined to showcase their products and techniques on *him*. A small patch of hair-removal wax on his forearm, mud that smelled like swamp gas on the back of his hand. And worse, the all-natural energizing spray with the aroma of mint and peaches that one of them had misted him with.

Kill me. Just kill me now. His brothers? Off taking the herd to high pasture for the next two days. Slippery bastards.

The trio of cheerful women sitting on the sofa right now made no qualms about blatantly flirting with him in front of his mother, who sat quietly with an amused grin. Levi rubbed his eyes. He had Agate Falls plans to work on today.

The phone call he'd had an hour ago, informing him that the survey crew was coming that morning, offered him a get-out-of-spa-hell card, but he didn't want to make his mother do this alone. He'd promised her, and his brothers, that he'd be involved, so he would. Even though it was sucking the manliness right out of him.

"What's the size of your current business space in Missoula?" He hoped his tone didn't display how edgy he was. "And do you feel it's adequate?"

The blonde, Misty, if he remembered right, batted her heavily mascaraed eyelashes. "May I have your hand, Mr. Haywood?" Without waiting for a response, she moved closer—got on her knees in front of him—and grabbed his hand. Settling between his parted knees, she leaned back on her haunches so her face came awfully close to places her face shouldn't be with his mother in the room. He scooted back in his chair.

Okay, so this could be a perk. The blonde was pretty, curvy, and filled out her tight T-shirt pretty damn well. And hell, she was on her knees looking up at him. If the expression on her face was any indication, she was interested. This should have made his heart flip or something. But her fingers didn't feel right. They were long and bony, with nails too long to be useful for anything more than decoration. When she flipped his hand over, his skin actually started to crawl. She might be attractive, but she wasn't Carrie.

No woman was Carrie.

"Wait until you feel this, Levi," she purred as if they were alone in the room, squeezing a dollop of brown goop onto his wrist, and she began rubbing it in. The heavy, sweet scent of chocolate filled the air. "Mmmm, feels good, right? It's our exclusive line of creamy massage oils. They'll make you feel amazing...and smell good enough to eat." The husky way the last word came out made his gut churn.

Levi drew his arm back. Enough. He didn't want to be touched. It had been hard enough letting Carrie do what she had the other night. Her hands on him had been surreal, amazing. Perfect. Humiliating. Even over his jeans, she had to have been able to feel how messed up his leg was. He squirmed in his seat. He needed air, and he needed this woman to get off her knees. "Thanks for the demo." She took the hint, rising with a plastic smile.

"So, about that square footage. How much would you need to open your spa division here on the ranch?" The rest of the interview went quickly. He barely noticed when the women gathered their things and left, his gaze drifting to the window as it had repeatedly throughout the morning. The sun was shining, the grass as green as he'd seen it yet, and he was itching to get out there and do something.

Truthfully, he hadn't felt this limber and light on his feet in recent memory. It was Carrie's doing, he was convinced. He kept playing it over and over in his mind, the way she worked the pain right out of him. Maybe it had been a fluke… just his body's reaction to being in her proximity after such a long time. She'd always had a way with touch and the ability to soothe, not only him, but others in pain as well. He was more inclined to think it was just *her*. And if so, he needed more.

"Levi." His mother's voice drew him back. She was standing next to his chair, looking tired and pale. He rose with immediate concern. How had he not paid more attention to her during the interviews? He might have noticed then that she looked exhausted. Suffering from multiple sclerosis, Maeve had good days and bad. Luckily the good had been winning recently. But planning her wedding in two weeks and helping with the guest services portion of Paint River was taking its toll.

"You should go lie down, Ma." When he gently took her arm, Maeve covered his hand and gave a good squeeze. Chronic disease did nothing to weaken her tough, independent resolve.

"I'm going to take you up on that." Maeve checked her watch. "But first, which candidate did you like the best?"

Levi stifled a groan. He'd been exfoliated, waxed,

slathered with dirt-colored, chocolate-scented cream, and had a strange woman's head between his legs. Limits. He had them.

"You don't really want me to answer that, Ma."

Her eyes twinkled as she patted his cheek. "You're right. I probably don't." She walked out of the living room and down the hall, leaving him to gather up his flannel jacket and swipe the lock screen on his cell phone. With any luck he'd be able to catch the survey team before they left. His brothers had been planning on putting in a campground on the ranch for a while, but they were out of space. Every encroachment of the tourist side into pasture ate away at Paint River's original purpose: raising cattle.

Utilizing Agate Falls' land could be beneficial— profitable—for them both. Darren had said he was open to possibilities, though preserving the land would be optimal. Levi wanted a clear plan before bringing it to Darren, and by proxy, Carrie, so they could weigh the pros and cons.

Levi rubbed a hand over his face as he flipped through the numbers in his cell. He knew she was nervous about his plans for the ranch, but it wasn't as if he'd be making all the decisions himself. Ultimately, it was about keeping Agate Falls operating, but he wanted to do right by her, too.

He paused in searching for the phone number. Even when they hadn't been together anymore, she'd been important to him. Thinking about her had gotten him through some tough shit, like gunfire over his head and long, anxious nights riddled with mortar fire—the day he'd almost died.

Everything he'd done, and everything he'd do now, was for her benefit. Because, God, he probably still cared about her more than he should. He probably still lov—

A door slammed.

"Levi Haywood, what the hell do you think you're doing?"

Chapter Six

Her voice lost velocity, because the moment Levi turned his innocent-looking smolder on her, she forgot how to function. Realizing her mouth was hanging open, Carrie pressed her lips together. She was tempted to ask him to step away from the light, on account that he looked like a freaking Greek god standing there, all swathed in a golden glow, and it was only making her angrier.

Black hair and chiseled face, broad shoulders, and huge biceps showing beneath his shirt. The gleam in his eyes made her pulse quicken. He moved to her side with purposeful steps as if his sole intent was making contact with her body. She held her breath just long enough for his fingers to slide gently over her upper arm. And then she exhaled with a quick, low whoosh, shivers racing down her arm at the caress of his hand.

"That's an interesting way to say hello, Carrie Lynn."

An overpoweringly sweet scent wafted off him. She wrinkled her nose and without thinking about it, leaned into him to take a better whiff. Common sense came rushing back and she moved away before she did something really stupid, like grab his bare arm and lick him. Slowly.

"Why do you smell like chocolate pudding?"

He gave a stunted laugh and moved his hand to his front pocket. "Is it that bad?"

"No, it's delicious." A flush heated her face even before the words were done tumbling out. Smoke replaced the light of humor in his eyes. Blinking hard, Carrie turned away from the glare from the window. It bothered her eyes...but also made a perfect excuse to put a little more distance between them. He moved along with her, keeping the proximity.

"Carrie." Levi's breath washed over the back of her neck, and the warm electric sparks down her spine didn't come from the sun. She could feel him there, his body, as he'd stepped up behind her. Her muscles tensed in preparation for his touch, but none came—both a blessing and a disappointment. "What can I do for you?"

"You can start by telling me why the hell a crew is taking measurements for a campground on Agate Falls land." She'd much prefer to talk to her dad about this, but since he was out and about, Levi was her only choice.

"Do you want to sit?" Levi moved beside her, creating a trail of chocolate-scented air.

"No."

He moved across the open living room and into the kitchen. "Soda?"

"Are you stalling, Levi?"

He sauntered back over with a can of Coke in one hand. "I don't have a reason to stall. And I'm not quite sure you have a reason to be so upset right now."

"Are you kidding me? Does my dad know that you're planning to tear up Agate Falls—?"

"Why do you think he wouldn't know?"

"So you are planning to develop the land? And what?

Turn it into another Paint River?"

Her own vitriol confused and shocked her. This wasn't her normal… She didn't let go of her emotions like this. Figuring it was a reaction to him and not so much the circumstances, she willed herself to cool it.

"It's business, Carrie. We're looking at options. Weighing choices that can bring long-term financial stability to Agate Falls. That's all."

"That's *not* all." Not by a long shot. Developing the ranch would mean changing it, taking away the landscape of her childhood. The adult part of her understood that nothing stayed the same, but the little girl inside wanted everything to stay the way she remembered it.

"Are you mad about the ranch, or is this about me and you?"

There was no way she was answering that, even if she already knew the answer. "There is no me and you."

"Damn it, you know what I mean."

Of course she did. Opening that can of worms wasn't worth the turmoil. Not when there couldn't be anything more between them than *business*, and soon, once she went back to Wyoming, nothing. "You think a lot of yourself if you're implying that I didn't put you out of my heart years ago." She lifted her chin. "The only thing between you and me right now is wanting what's best for Agate Falls, even if we don't have the same ideas in mind."

"I'm the boss, Carrie."

"Excuse me?"

"Fifty-five percent. That's how much stake I hold in Agate Falls, which means, technically, I own it." He cracked the can and took a drink. "Look, I won't keep anything from you. You're a part of Agate Falls, and…you're important."

She shrugged off his comment, though it gave her a trickle of warmth. The flash of angst she'd had about this whole thing suddenly seemed like an overinflated knee-jerk reaction. In the big picture, she didn't have much say in how things went. She lived a state away, had her own life off the ranch. What her dad and Levi decided to do wouldn't be ruled by her nostalgia and need to hang on.

Her reluctance to let go and the ever-growing secret wish that she could stay were having a tug-of-war. It was hard to let go of the past when she was so scared about her future. Still, it was her problem. Not Levi's.

Deflated, she could only nod. "Thank you." Feeling incredibly silly, she moved to go, but his voice stopped her.

"Look, what you did for me the other night...the leg thing. Thank you."

"You're welcome." In the four years she'd been working as a massage therapist, she'd never been as grateful for her skills as she had the other night. Easing Levi out of his misery had been profoundly satisfying. Witnessing his complete and utter agony had pulled a primal instinct from somewhere inside her to fix it.

"How did you know what to do?"

"Hmmm?" She turned to look at him while moving farther away from the sunlight. Dots and shards of light danced inside her right eye. She closed her eyes and pressed fingers to her lids, cursing, for the millionth time, this change that was happening to her.

"Oh, I'm a chiropractic assistant. I do massage, sometimes."

When she opened her eyes, she noticed he was watching her intently...too intently. "I've had massages before."

"Oh?"

"As part of my therapy. But none of them ever came close to what you did." Levi moved closer. "It was a little magical, actually."

"Magical," she repeated, watching him advance. The

tension between them was both sweet and disconcerting, and she wished the slightly awkward, uncomfortable thing would go away. Then again, it helped remind her that she wasn't here on a personal level.

Time had given the lines and edges of his face a maturity that heightened his masculine appeal. And no doubt the military had provided him with the razor-sharp and completely breath-stealing expression. Even in the dimmer cast of light, his eyes glowed with intensity that shot a throb between her legs and a flicker of apprehension in her breast.

He stopped, close enough that heat radiated from his chest to hers. Around his neck, a silver chain disappeared beneath his shirt. It didn't take much to guess what the chain held, and she wanted to see. She touched her fingertips to his collarbone, exhaling as if the contact were the fuel she needed to breathe, tracing the chain and slowly pulling it until a single dog tag slid up from beneath the fabric.

His name was stamped into it, the metal tarnished on one edge as if it had been rubbed repeatedly. The tag rested in her palm, warm from his body heat. One small, thin piece of metal represented the different paths they'd taken. She'd held his tags before, though he wouldn't remember. She'd thought then, as she did now, what a strong, admirable man he was. Levi Haywood was a damn good man.

She let go, and the tag clanked against the chain as she stepped back. "I'm sorry. I shouldn't have…"

"You never have to apologize for touching me, Carrie." Low, almost dangerous, the tone sent a sensual ripple through her body. "In fact, I'd like you do it again, right now."

Her gaze fell to his lips as her palm met his chest. Carrie took one small step forward, pressing her hand flat again and traveling it over his pecs, the fabric of his shirt sliding over his firm, warm muscle, to his ribs where his torso stiffened and his breath stalled. Lightly, he gripped her wrist in one hand and tipped her chin with the other. Her mind and body seemed to go somewhere else, a static place, where this moment erased everything else.

He swept a thumb over her lower lip. "We have unfinished business."

She shook her head, trying to dissuade him, herself; both. In a couple weeks she'd be gone—would be reduced to seeing Levi once or twice a year when she came home to visit, maybe. That wasn't really worth the emotional wringer she'd have to go through if she let herself get close to him.

"We don't."

"We do."

"No." She shook her head again, the sting behind her eyes biting. If this moment could truly be suspended and molded into whatever she wanted it to be, there *would* be a second chance. Her vision and health would be perfect, and she could safely live in this remote place. But her future wasn't malleable. And a second chance wasn't possible.

"Maybe you have unfinished stuff, but I don't, and I'd rather you didn't bring it up again."

His head dipped low. Her lips began to tingle and want. With the touch of his breath, her mouth parted. He drew closer.

"Sounds like a challenge, Carrie. Remember what happens when you challenge me?"

She studied the faint kiss of freckles across his nose, the angle of his cheekbones and strength of his smooth jaw. The beauty of it muddled her thoughts...until she remembered that she couldn't do this. If he kissed her, she'd want more.

Carrie stepped back, immediately regretting the loss of his closeness. "Yes, I do. You usually lose."

A low chuckle sounded from deep in his throat, the reverberation of it giving her goose bumps. "Never lost your spirit, did you, Sunshine?" The nickname tugged at her heart. It was another connection, like a puzzle piece falling into place.

Carrie glanced up, her forehead going tight with the sudden realization that Levi was the common thread in her deep-seated need to be here, surrounded by family and familiar faces. If she didn't get control of whatever was going on between them right now, she was going to fall. Hard. Wallowing in self-pity over what she couldn't have wasn't an appealing thought. She did too much of that as it was.

"Look, my granddaddy's barn is on that land. I don't know what my father is thinking, but he'd never want it torn down." She reached in her pocket for her truck keys, trying hard to get her in-control side back into place.

He groaned. "This again? No one is taking down the barn." He crossed his arms, feet wide like a military guard standing over something important. "Nothing is set in stone, and we don't have to develop that exact location. That's why the survey crew is there, so we can look at options. Which reminds me." He pulled his cell from his pocket and looked at it. "I'm about out of time to catch them before they go. This has been fun, but you'll have to excuse me."

Levi indicated the door with a sweep of his arm. Suddenly sluggish, Carrie realized it was well past noon and she hadn't eaten or taken her insulin. She'd been a little fatigued this morning but attributed it to not sleeping well. No way did she want to push it, even though she was tempted to go with Levi to meet the crew. Food, medicine, and a nap would dictate the rest of her day.

Descending the porch steps, she opened her truck door and looked back at him. "Good-bye, Levi."

His grin was huge, infuriating, as he walked behind her to go to his own vehicle. His hand traced her lower back as he passed. "How about, 'until later'? Because trust me, Sunshine, we're nowhere near done."

Chapter Seven

The sun was struggling to wake up when Levi pulled into Agate Falls to help with their branding. Even through his flannel shirt and denim jacket, the chill tugged at his arms and the backs of his shoulders with a damp undertone that spoke of a brewing storm. He found Darren in the cattle barn. The older man handed him a mug of steaming coffee and they got to work gathering rope, veterinary supplies, and other odds and ends. Cowboys had gone out to herd the cattle from the high pasture down to the branding pens. Any time now, other ranchers would show up and they could get started.

He just wasn't into it today. His legs ached something terrible. Levi sucked it up and drained his coffee. Branding should go quickly, considering Agate Falls had fewer cattle than Paint River. He should probably take it easy today, but the thought of being idle made him restless. There was too much going on in his mind to go slow.

"The survey went well," he told Darren. "I should hear back from them in a week or so with the full report."

Darren nodded. "That's good." A few ranch hands went

in and out. Half expecting Carrie to come walking in at any moment, Levi glanced to the door. She'd always loved branding. When they were younger, they'd ride out with the men early in the morning to round up the cattle and bring them to the pens. When her health got tricky, she'd do small things like help with lunch, or simply stand at the rails and watch. He'd always felt sorry for her that she couldn't be riding and in the middle of the action, but she never complained.

"Carrie come to see you yesterday?" Darren asked quietly, almost as if he'd been reading Levi's mind.

Levi grabbed a metal toolbox and added it to his pile to carry outside. "Yes, sir."

"What did you tell her?"

That was a loaded question, depending on what exactly he was talking about. They'd slung a lot of words around yesterday and damn if he hadn't almost kissed her. When she'd pulled his dog tag out of his shirt and held it in her palm, he'd nearly come undone. Emotions had flickered across her face in that moment, from sadness to anger to something that had looked a lot like regret. He'd felt each poignantly as they'd stood connected by that slip of metal.

"I told her the truth about the survey crew. She'd seen them and asked me about it. I'm surprised the two of you hadn't already talked about things, though."

Darren turned back to his work. "I was going to the other night, but she wasn't feeling well. She went to bed early." Before Levi could ask, the older man threw him a look over his shoulder. "She'll be fine. Just a medication change is all."

Levi didn't respond. How many times had he been with her when her blood sugar went low and she'd needed help? Countless. As she'd grown and her body started to adjust, things evened out and she stopped having so many problems.

But diabetes was a lifelong condition, and hers was hard to regulate. The doctors had told her early on that she'd always struggle and have to be vigilant.

He'd been vigilant with her, and so had her father. Always watching. Always worrying. He'd hoped over the years that things would get easier for her, that her body would find a rhythm with an insulin that worked well. Seemed as if she might still be struggling a bit, though.

"That's good." Levi pulled a pair of gloves from his back pocket and slipped into them with the sudden urge to go check on her. She'd probably roll her eyes and order him out. It had been a little heated between them when they'd parted ways yesterday. He refilled his coffee from a thermos on the ground and did the same for Darren.

"I know it was hard on you, Levi, what you did back then for me. I hope you realize that getting Carrie off the ranch and into college in the city is what she needed."

The mug wobbled in his hand. Levi gripped it hard. Hardly a day had gone by that he didn't wonder what life would have been like if he hadn't listened to Darren all those years ago and, instead of leaving Carrie behind, asked her to go with him. Sometimes the images in his head were good ones—her waiting at the military base for him when he returned from deployment, having her at his side as often as possible.

Mostly, though, he ruminated on how hard the life of a military spouse would have been on her. She'd have been alone, in a strange place far from home, moving as soon as it began to feel familiar. Always waiting on him, and him always worrying that she was healthy and safe while he was gone.

Sending Carrie to Wyoming to live with her aunts had been a smart plan. There she had people to watch over her while she went to college. He couldn't be her protector, her lover, when he was thousands of miles away for months at a time. No, as much as he regretted everything they'd lost, he wouldn't change anything. Pushing her away had been the right thing to do.

A low hum started in his ears. "Yeah," he heard himself respond. Life on a ranch wouldn't have been safe for Carrie any more than life as a military wife.

"She'll be going back to Wyoming soon." Darren threw a hay bale and pushed it into place with his knee. "No sense in getting her too wrapped up in the changes going on around here. Being stressed and all ain't good for her blood sugar."

She'd always been a spitfire, quick-tempered and stubborn as all hell. Considering how she'd come to see him, mad as could be, things hadn't changed much. Levi swallowed his irritation and wiped a forearm over his face. No good ever came from keeping her in the dark—it just upset her more. And why shouldn't it?

They weren't kids anymore. She was a grown woman, and he was going to treat her like one. That included keeping her in the loop like she'd asked him to. He hitched a leg and cranked his head back to stretch out some of the tension that had gathered across his shoulders.

Darren took off his hat and ran a hand over his silver hair. "I suppose the two of you'll have a few things to say to each other, too. Just as long as you keep in mind that she's *going back* to Wyoming." The icy glare in the older man's eyes cut Levi deep and pissed him off equally.

"Whatever happens between your daughter and me is our business." Levi pulled off his gloves. "What happens here at Agate Falls in *our* business." He pointed between himself and Darren. "That's the way it's going to be. Sir." He squared his shoulders, waiting for whatever response Darren might throw his way. Did he want to clear the air with Carrie about their past? Of course. Didn't mean he was looking forward to it, or had illusions about things being anything but friendly for them. He was well aware she had a life in Wyoming, and it was her choice if she wanted to go back to it or not. Really, he had no idea what she wanted—not yet.

Darren gave him a sideways glance before nodding and turning back to his work. "Fair enough."

Two short words, but they ended the conversation amicably. He might be Agate Falls' investor, but Darren was still his elder and he respected the man. He had no desire to go head-to-head with him.

Voices from outside drew Levi's attention, especially the feminine one mixed with the deeper male tones.

"How much fence?" Carrie's voice was soft and sleepy as she walked in with two ranch hands at her side. Immersed in conversation with the man next to her, she didn't seem to notice Levi at first. The cowboy leaned in as if telling her a secret, and she smiled. Levi clenched his jaw, grinding his molars so hard a shot of pain went straight up to his temple. He tucked a rag he'd been using into his back pocket and walked over to them.

He turned to the cowboy, whose name he couldn't remember, and looked him up and down. If the man got any closer to Carrie, Levi was going to have to pile-drive him. "What's going on?"

The cowboy shifted so his arm brushed Carrie's, the challenging look in his eye saying he knew exactly what he was doing. "Broken fence on the high pasture. Didn't have time to check real good, since we had to get the cattle down here, but we'll go back up as soon as—"

"No." Grabbing a huge length of looped rope, he shoved it into the man's chest. Satisfied when the cowboy lost contact with Carrie, Levi waved toward the door. "You can start taking this stuff out. I'll take care of the fence." The man sniffed loudly, his face going hard. Too bad. He could flirt on his own time.

Just not with Carrie.

She moved toward her father, brushing past Levi with a curious sideways glance.

"Can't let it go too long, and rain's moving in," Darren said.

"I'll go now. My brothers will be here any time to help in the pens." Checking the fence gave him an option that would be easier on his body and still be physical enough to make the time go by.

"I'll go, too." Carrie pulled a knit hat over her head, then moved to the thermos and poured her dad another cup of coffee.

"Don't be ridiculous." Darren accepted the mug. "Levi can manage."

"I said, I'll go." The firm snap in her voice made every man jump to attention. Now, *there* was a challenge. Levi eyed Darren, who was eyeing Carrie like he wanted to strap her down to a chair.

"I feel fine and don't be assuming otherwise." She shifted her weight from one foot to the other, holding her dad's gaze with a deliberate lack of expression. He couldn't recall ever seeing her poker face before, but this was impressive. With a sudden burst of protectiveness, Levi moved beside her. If the girl wanted to do more than serve lunch today, so be it.

"Let's saddle up."

Chapter Eight

The burn in her thighs was nothing compared to the joy in Carrie's heart. She hadn't ridden in a few years, and her legs were reminding her now. Relaxing into the saddle as the sun hovered above the horizon, she figured not being able to walk for a few days was totally worth it. Tiny dots floated in and out of her vision, a common occurrence that usually frustrated her. Right now, she wasn't going to let it. There was too much in this moment to savor—the gorgeous pink-and-yellow sky, the vibrant green of the foliage. The sexy cowboy riding next to her. She rubbed her eyes and put on a pair of sunglasses. They'd cut the glare and hide how much she couldn't stop peeking at Levi. Hopefully.

He hadn't said much since they'd left the ranch, but he seemed comfortable enough that she'd tagged along. She hadn't intended to, until his little display of jealousy in the barn. Maybe he still had feelings for her, or maybe just being together again drummed up a lot of old emotions. They needed to talk—she couldn't put it off anymore—to get to know each other again, so maybe, they could part friends this time.

Friends. Could they ever really be a part of each other's lives? It was a question she'd played with since running into him at May Fire. The heat in Levi's eyes over the way the cowboy had spoken low and intimately to her had been surprising, yet filled her with a girlie sense of satisfaction. There hadn't been another man yet who could fill her with such sweet anticipation and want. *Don't go there.*

They'd just talk, start small. Take it from there.

"Must be some heavy thoughts on your mind." Levi moved his horse a little closer to hers. A burst of sunlight illuminated beside him, making his inky hair shine.

"Yeah? What tipped you off?"

"Your face is all scrunched up." He remembered her tics, could probably still read her like an open book.

"Just admiring the beauty." One side of her mouth tugged up. Subtle. Levi reached for her, pinching a long curl of her hair between his fingers and giving it a gentle pull.

"Funny. So was I." He twirled the strand, once, twice, before letting it fall.

"I came to see you," she blurted, wishing he'd touch her again, but hoping that he didn't. If he did, she might trade a seat on her horse for one on his, with her body wrapped around him. She had so many residual emotions tied to him, and she didn't know what to do with any of them. Get close, stay away. What did you do with desires and feelings that had no clear place?

"What? When?"

Her grip tightened on the reins. "December," she whispered. "In the hospital." She usually avoided dredging up memories, but she had a sense of calm about it right now.

"Tucker and I, well, we texted back and forth now and then. He kept me updated on how you were...you know, after you and I stopped writing." She considered stopping there, but she'd already gone this far. "The day after you were brought to Missoula General, I came and sat with you a while." She'd laid her head next to his on the pillow, wanting like hell to crawl into the bed and hold him, but all the tubes and wires on his body prevented it. She'd found his dog tags on the bedside table, and held them between her palms for so long that they imprinted her skin.

Levi stared ahead quietly. The sky darkened as heavy clouds passed through. In the long silence, she thought maybe she'd been better off keeping the confession to herself.

He flipped up the collar on his jacket as another burst of wind came through. "I wish I could remember it."

"You were a little out of it." To put it mildly.

"Sorry I wasn't better company." His tone was heavy despite the good-natured quip.

"I just wanted you to know." She did feel lighter for having said it, as if taking this first step is exactly what her clogged-up soul needed. When he didn't respond, she dropped it. Unless he'd gotten better about deep conversations, he'd talk when he was ready. If she pushed, he'd clam up.

Looking to the sky, she gauged how much longer until they got to the north point. Levi's horse made a bunny-hop, tossing his head and prancing high. He spoke softly, patting the horse on the neck until the animal was settled. They rode in silence, a companionable air falling between them that reminded Carrie of how it used to be. How sweet it would be to simply slip back into the old rhythm they'd had, Levi at her side, doing most everything together because they enjoyed each other's company. Making plans. Making love.

They rode up a rocky path, the sky getting darker as they went. She pulled off her sunglasses and tucked them in a pocket, glad to find she could see pretty well in the faded light.

Levi cut in front of her as the incline became steeper, the

path narrower. She shifted in the saddle to give her aching bottom some relief.

"Up here." He pointed ahead as they cleared the top of a rise. The ground beneath them was well trampled, hoofprints showing this was where the men had been earlier. They rode a little farther until the fence came into view.

"Well, here we go." Levi dismounted and handed Carrie the reins. A long section of fence had the top two strands broken. He inspected the damage and came back over for the repair supplies strapped to the back of his saddle. "Clean breaks and the posts are fine. Won't take long to splice these together."

A light mist fell, coating her face and the pieces of hair twining around her hat. A low rumble started in the air, making them both glance up.

"Why don't you stay here and watch the horses? I'll work fast." He left before she could respond, but she wasn't going to argue. The fence didn't look bad enough to require two people to fix, and he'd be more efficient at the task anyway. Another rumble disturbed the air, followed by a loud crack. Levi's horse jumped, his shoulder bumping into her knee. She held the reins tight and gripped the saddle with her thighs to keep her balance. She spoke softly, patting his neck until he settled.

As minutes ticked by, the mist turned to slow rain, dropping a steady blip, blip, blip onto her head. She relaxed some, listening to sounds of Levi working in the distance mixed with the grumbling sky. A gust of wind rattled the trees and called up a swirl of dried leaves from the ground. Next to her, Levi's horse trembled. She was surprised he was so skittish. Her dad's horses were usually bulletproof, but this guy had some kinks to work out.

Another blast of wind followed the first, blowing small twigs and leaves from the branches. A few pieces fell onto the horse's heads, bringing Levi's gelding to his breaking point. His neck and shoulder muscles tensed. Carrie tried to brace herself by getting hold of the saddle horn. Slamming into the side of her horse, Levi's gelding reared up, his hooves nearly striking her leg. Both horses jerked, her own swinging his butt sideways, back hooves skidding in the dirt.

She yelped, trying to hang on, but she'd been too relaxed. Burning pain lanced beneath her ribs as she twisted, and started to fall. Strong hands grabbed around her middle. Momentum won, launching her down onto Levi, forcing him back until he landed on the ground with a grunt. Her chest slamming onto his. It took her a moment to realize what happened. With a start, she looked for the horses, sure they were about to be trampled, but the geldings had moved off together near the base of a huge oak tree.

Tension in her chest made it hard to breathe, and when she looked down at Levi, it got worse. The top of his coat and the flannel shirt underneath gaped, showing a deep triangle of dusky skin and the dip between his collarbones. The masculine line of his neck and jaw were dusted with dark stubble. It was a little darker around his mouth, creating a frame for lips she wanted so badly to taste.

"You okay?" His fingers gripped her sides, holding her close. "Okay" was relative. Was she fine from the fall that he buffered? Sure. Was she okay right now, lying on his rock-hard body, wishing he'd roll her over and...

"Yes." With a huff, she tried to push herself up, but looking at his lips again pulled her strength away. "...no."

Water ran off her hat and sprinkled around him, his face wet and his hair plastered to his head. She wiped a drop of rain from his eyelashes. "I'm not okay."

"Something I can fix?" His hands made a slow caress to the dip in her back. Her palms found his chest and pressed against the damp fabric that separated her hands from his flesh. Her lips tingled at the proximity of his delicious mouth; her fingers ached to get beneath fabric to find firm, warm male skin.

"Yes."

"I was hoping you'd say that." Levi lifted his upper body, one hand finding the back of her neck, urging her toward him. Her breath came tight, fast until it stalled completely as his long fingers threaded into her hair, knocking off her hat, and kneaded a fistful against her scalp. His mouth was in perfect alignment with hers, parted just a bit as if waiting for her to make a move. She had the urge to tell him that he'd always been the thread that stitched up all the troubles in her life. There was something to be said for having that one person beside you who made life, life. Right now, he was causing a rush of adrenaline that made her skin come alive with anticipation of his touch.

"Kiss me, Carrie." He didn't give her time to overthink it—think at all—as he pressed his lips to hers. The sparks of it wrenching a quick, surprised moan from her throat. The soft touch of flesh flashed into a desperate, raw kiss, his hand gripping her hair, his tongue meeting hers in a sensual slide. Levi's taste blossomed with familiarity, the sound he made as he urged her lips wide and deepened the kiss, one that had haunted her dreams.

Above them, the sky let loose, rain pummeling down, beating into Carrie's back and soaking her through. A tremor went through her, not from the cold, but from the heat between their bodies and the intimate way he held her.

His teeth raked her lower lip as he pulled back, breathing hard. "Damn, girl." A sexy grin pulled one corner of his mouth.

"Damn, cowboy." She tried to smile in return, but her face seemed frozen. Levi cupped her cheek, his brow falling as he ran a thumb under her eye. Carrie blinked fast, feeling wetness drop from her lashes. Rain…just rain. His fingers kneaded into her side, a comforting gesture she figured, but it cut into her flesh like he was poking a bruise. She winced, pulling away, realizing that something had happened when she'd twisted on the horse.

"What is it?" Levi set her carefully away, wiping water from her face, and then his.

"I'm fine. Just twisted too much when I fell, I think." Carrie pushed to her feet, taking the hand he offered. She steadied herself, still whirling from the kiss, and then turned toward him. Levi's eyelids fell halfway as he shifted, moving his arms apart. All she had to do was step into them and lose herself in his touch. Suddenly, a crack of thunder shook the sky, making her jump and the horses squeal. Levi put an arm around her shoulders and pulled her against his side protectively.

"Wow, that was close." She straightened, realizing she'd hunched down a bit against his chest. They waited a few moments before walking toward the horses. Her gelding recovered and stood calmly, but Levi's pranced and sidestepped. Before he could get closer, the horse spun and bolted, leaving them to stare at the sight of his retreating butt.

Levi grabbed Carrie's horse by the reins with a curse. "Your dad mentioned that horse was bipolar."

She snickered, and he followed suit. Ridiculous, but funny in frustrating way. The horse would run home while they were stranded in the downpour. She could only imagine how her father would freak out when the horse came galloping in, rider-less.

"This way," Carrie called through the rush of rain. Her vision blurred in the dim light as she picked her way through the trees and up an incline. She was relieved to see she'd recalled the spot correctly from her time up here as a kid. Ahead, a rocky overhang topped a dip in the hill, creating a crevice with a roof. Shivering almost uncontrollably, she picked her way toward the shelter. Levi followed and, leaving the horse just outside, he scooted in.

There was just enough room for them to stand side by side, Levi ducking to avoid hitting his head. "There," Carrie huffed, blowing onto her cupped fingers. "This is a little better, huh?" She lowered her hands and shook her arms to try to warm them, stopping dead when she glanced at Levi… and saw him unbuttoning his shirt.

Chapter Nine

Carrie was about to shake out of her skin. Her teeth were actually chattering. He shouldn't have agreed to let her come up here with him. If she ended up with pneumonia or something, he'd never forgive himself.

His oiled canvas jacket was mostly waterproof, the fleece lining inside warm and dry. He slipped out of it and put it between his knees, then unbuttoned his flannel and peeled it off.

"Take off your shirt." He gave her a look, knowing she was going to argue. She'd always been good at that. She crossed her arms, but he didn't give her time to be squirrely. "Take it off, or I will. Your bra, too." Her mouth parted, reminding him just how fantastic her lips had tasted. Dang, had that really happened? It seemed so surreal, to have her in his arms again...that taste so ripe on his lips.

"I'm not getting naked in front of you." Yeah, because that had never, ever happened before. He still remembered, vividly.

"Then turn around. Just do it before you freeze." His

breath came out in a puff, the temperature having dropped with the rain and wind. In a short-sleeved Henley, the cold air assaulted his bare arms, making him shiver. If he was this chilly dry, she had to be downright frozen. Gently, he gripped her shoulder. "Come on, Sunshine. Do as I say."

Her back stiffened but she didn't protest, just unzipped her coat and shrugged it off into a wet, heavy lump on the ground. A thin blue shirt molded the feminine structure of her back and into the dip of her spine. Levi traced her curves with his gaze. She unbuttoned her shirt and pulled it back, but it clung to her shoulders. With one hand, he grasped the neckline and pulled it down...slowly, the tip of his middle finger making a trail over her damp skin as he slid the shirt off.

Stepping closer, Levi was torn over wanting to pull her cold body into the warmth of his chest. The rain beat staccato on the rocks above, the patter splashing into the wet ground. Tracing her white satiny bra across her back, he grinned as a violent shudder went through her. How easy would it be to rekindle the fire between them? Not just this—though her form was something he wanted to explore slowly, intimately—but her heart, her mind. To know her again, all of her—how sweet would it be?

Letting her shirt drop, Levi used both hands to unhook the bra and toss it aside. Her arms came across her chest, the quick glance she tossed over her shoulder cautious. Levi settled his flannel shirt over her shoulders, held it in place as she shakily slid into it. He could tell that she was fumbling with the buttons, so he turned her to help. Slowly closing each button, thanks to his cold hands, he tried not to focus on the rise of her breasts beneath the fabric. Her chest went still and he swore she was holding her breath.

The chemistry was still there. Holy shit, was it still there, and he wanted to grab hold of it and see how far it went. How would he ever keep his shit together as she walked out of his life? Levi ran his palms over the tops of her shoulders, down her arms. What if he asked her for a second chance? What would she say?

Could he ask her to consider it…to give it a try?

Hell, he was being selfish. Look at her, shivering her beautiful ass off, pale face, blue-tinged lips. This environment wasn't safe for her—she'd left the ranch for a reason. Her diabetes was too unpredictable and he'd been a fool to endanger her today. Disgusted with himself, Levi helped her slide into his jacket, pulling it closed a little rougher than he needed to. Her hands clasped over his and he realized just then how quiet she'd been.

"God, Carrie, I'm sorry." He pulled her into his arms, encouraging her face to find his chest. "Let's get you warmed up."

"I'm fine."

"No, you're stubborn. There's a difference." He rubbed her back with his hands. "You know," he said, "there were so many times I wished for cold like this. Out there, in the desert…it got so hot you could have fried a steak on the ground."

She huffed a small laugh and it warmed him. Good. Not only would Darren kill him if anything happened to her, he'd kick his own ass. He should do it anyway for not being more prepared in case the weather turned. So much for a simple, quick ride to fix a fence.

"I'm glad you're home, Levi." The words touched him like a caress. Emotion lodged in his chest. He'd put her through a lot, and not a day had gone by that he didn't think about how to make it up to her somehow. Freezing her to death wasn't the way. This was just a reminder why he had to keep his hands to himself.

No more kissing—kissing might lead to more, and there

couldn't be more. Friends only. No more putting her in harm's way, even if it was just rain. He held her more tightly, rolling around the sweet scent of her hair and the feel of her pressed against him. Long minutes passed in which her shivering stopped and she relaxed, her cheek a warm imprint over his heart. Their connection was bittersweet. He'd longed for this, but now that he had it, he knew he had to let it go.

"Rain's stopping," he murmured as the downpour receded to intermittent drips. Reluctant to release her, Levi peered out from under the overhang where a break in the clouds uncovered a patch of blue. "Looks like it's moving on. We should go."

He moved to check the horse's saddle and wipe away as much water from the leather as he could. Holding her clothes, Carrie mounted the horse and Levi swung up behind her. It was a tight fit that pressed his thighs against the backs of hers, contact that had him buzzing. Ignoring the sensation, he guided the horse down the hill and headed toward the ranch.

He wanted to make small talk, but silence felt better. He enjoyed the feel of her close to his body, while still concentrating on the land. She didn't seem in any hurry to talk, either. She'd stopped shaking, her warmth making the cool air a little more tolerable for him, to the point where this was almost nice. Comfortable. Another memory he'd cherish in the days to come when she was gone.

• • •

"What do you mean, you're leaving?" Carrie set down the wooden spoon in her hand and turned to her father. Darren filled his coffee mug slowly, as if he could postpone having to elaborate. Putting the carafe away, he leaned against the kitchen counter next to her. Warm and dry after a hot shower and fresh clothes, she'd heated up the stew and bread she'd made the day before and took it out to feed the crew. The men had waited out the rain and then gotten back to branding. Stopping just long enough to wolf down the food, the men were back at it.

"Got a rancher in Colorado interested in one of our bulls and some breeding stock. He's paying higher prices than what I can get here. If he likes 'em, he'll buy more." He took a long draw of his coffee. "He called me while you were out there getting rained on."

So far, this trip home had left them with a lot of work to do and little time for talking. In a snap, her time here would be up and she'd be leaving, without ever getting to anything meaningful. He had asked *her* to come home for a visit, after all. Turning to reach a plastic container, she winced against pain that lanced beneath her ribs. Her dad set down his cup and immediately reached out a hand.

"What's wrong?"

Carrie waved him off. He was always so quick to find a reason to ban her from doing anything but lie around and bore herself to death. "Just pulled a muscle when I fell off the horse."

The coffee mug slammed down. "You *fell off* a horse? Goddamn it, Levi is—"

Carrie picked up his mug and handed it back to him with a sigh. Home a few days and here it was, the overprotecting bullshit. "Levi kept me warm and safe. And you need to stop worrying so much." She pointed the spoon at him. "And he fixed your fence, so be happy." She'd tried to give him back his jacket at lunchtime, but he'd refused. He'd accepted the flannel shirt, though, but kept it unbuttoned as if he welcomed the chill. Hot-blooded, that man. Her face flushed at the thought.

Her dad scoffed and swirled his mug, watching the liquid slosh around. "His fence."

"What?"

"*His* fence. All this, everything, is his." He waved a hand around, the tension in his voice heavy in her ears. "I messed up, Carrie-girl, and I had to have a Haywood come save me." Shoving her ponytail over one shoulder, she leaned against the counter, hip-to-hip with him.

"All I have left is you. I did this because I didn't want you to look at me and see failure—hate me because the ranch was gone. It's going to be…gone, anyway. Mostly."

She gripped his wrist tenderly, searching his face until he looked at her. "Dad, I'd never hate you. Things happen, things you don't expect or can't really prepare for, so you do what you have to."

He gave a sarcastic grunt. "Develop the land?"

She couldn't imagine Agate Falls as a tourist spot any more today than before. The thought of it left a huge, queasy hole in her gut. "Tell Levi no. Tell him you don't want that stupid campground on your land." He opened his mouth but she shook her head. "*Your* land, because you're going to pay off his investment and get ownership back. You will."

Deep lines furrowed her father's forehead, the crow's feet around his eyes like cracks in the sand. Worn and defeated, the disappointment in his heart was clear. Carrie put her hand over his, wishing fiercely that she could stay and support him. Be his rock, like she'd been for so many years. Inside the strong heart of a workingman was the lead weight of pride, and his had fallen. Hard.

She *could* stay. The thought gave her pause. It wasn't completely out of the question, was it? The thought came and went, and Carrie dismissed it before it could bloom. The little dots that floated around her left eye like relentless polka dots were reminder enough why she couldn't stay. Diabetes aside, at some point, she'd lose her ability to drive, to be independent. What then?

Putting away the thought and the sting of regret, she poured herself a cup of coffee and held the warm ceramic between both hands. "What other plans does Levi have for the ranch?" There had to be options, other things they could investigate.

"Looking at some herd management things. Maybe bring in some new stock. Mostly, he's looking at long-term cash flow that isn't directly tied to the beef market." His tone was less than enthusiastic, as if he didn't believe anything else would work out. She wondered if Levi was pushing for the campground at the expense of other valid ideas. Didn't it make sense to preserve the land as much as possible? The Haywoods made their fortune by selling luxury to outsiders, and they were paying for it now by maxing out their land capacity—or they wouldn't be after Agate Falls' space.

"Granddaddy would spit in your eye if he knew you were thinking of developing the land." He'd cherished his chew like a prize, always tucking a bit away in his lip and keeping the rest in his front shirt pocket, just like her dad had done until he'd quit a few years back. The comment drew a smile that made his eyes sparkle.

"Yes, ma'am, he would. Good thing he's not here right now, isn't it?" Her heart fell at his reply. She worried that he wouldn't refuse the campground if it came right down to it. She needed to talk to Levi some more and find out just what other plans he had up his sleeve. She set down her mug and began scooping the leftovers into a container.

She'd been *alone* with Levi this morning. Soaking wet, safe in his arms. Warm…and tingly and tight with anticipation when he'd kissed her. That scorching kiss, with her body pressed against his, the rise and fall of his chest under her breasts, had driven an electrifying spark though her that she hadn't felt in, well, ever. That alone made the idea of hanging around tempting.

And ridiculous. Rolling her eyes at her own foolishness, Carrie put a lid on the container and her wayward fantasies. "How long will you be gone?"

"Couple days. I'm heading out tomorrow morning. Levi will have everything under control here while I'm gone." Buying and selling cattle had always been her dad's thing. Being on the road with his truck and stock trailer was like Christmas for him, so she wasn't surprised that he hadn't pawned this trip off on someone else. "I'll be calling you three times a day and Levi or one of the Haywood women will be by every day to check in with you."

"Okay." She wiped her hands on a dish towel before turning to put her arms around him. There was no sense in reminding him that her diabetes had been good to her lately and she hadn't had a low in months. He'd worry anyway.

"I'm going back to work before they come looking for me." He gave her a tender smile and grabbed his hat from the table before walking out. Carrie cleaned up the kitchen, ruminating on the things they'd talked about, trying to drum up new ideas that might help the ranch. Except that her mind kept straying to Levi and that morning, and the way her body had lit up with his touch.

Getting out some cleaner, she doused the countertop and scrubbed until her arm and the hitch in her side started to throb. When that was done, she turned to the sink, and then the cupboard doors. Cleaning worked the knots out of her thoughts, and right now, thanks to Levi, she had a lot of them.

She'd just filled a bucket to scrub the floor when the back of her neck tingled. Pausing to listen, she heard the distant noise of bellowing cattle and shouting men. She almost shrugged it off and went back to her work, but something made her stop and hold her breath. It was faint over the other noise…

A voice calling her name.

Chapter Ten

"Carrie?"

Unsure at first where it was coming from, she crossed to the kitchen door. Her dad must have left it cracked open when he'd gone out. A shape at the bottom of the porch steps gave her a jolt.

"Hey, can you toss my jacket out here?" Levi's voice was tight, tense, followed with a low grunt as if he were trying to hold back pain.

"Come on in and let me find it." She'd rearranged the table and chairs and moved things out of the way in preparation for mopping the floor. She had no idea where she'd put it.

"I'll wait." There it was again, words punctuated with a groan as if talking was difficult. Wiping her hands on her jeans, she pushed open the screen door and went out. It took a minute for her eyes to adjust in the light, but she saw clearly enough to read the hard-etched lines on his face.

"You get kicked or something?"

Levi was bracing himself with one arm on the railing, bent over a little. "No. Get my jacket, please?" She started toward him, but he put his other hand out at her, palm up. "Damn it, woman, don't."

His harsh tone stopped her, surprise turning into irritation with a big helping of concern. Then she realized he'd been on a horse all day, like the last time he'd had pain. His legs. Snapped back into motion, she went to the top step and looked down, offering him a hand even though he wouldn't be able to reach it from down there.

"Let me help you. Come on."

"Fuck, Carrie. I said, *don't.*"

"And I said, come on." She extended her hand again, knowing full well that he wouldn't come up to take it. It ripped her up inside to see him like this, and as long as she had the ability to help, she'd push him until he accepted or stormed off. By the agonized look on his face, he wasn't in the position to be storming off anywhere.

Levi looked up, fading daylight casting his face in gray. His breath came hard and soft, once, twice, four times until he blinked and set his jaw. "Go inside. I won't come up with you standing there."

Men and their pride. Fine. As her own disability progressed, Carrie often wondered what it would be like to have to rely on others for help, and if her self-worth would suffer because of it. For Levi, needing help was probably about the worst blow imaginable.

A minute or so later, Levi came in, so pale she thought he was going to pass out. She ushered him into the living room. His broad shoulders were set tight, pulling his shirt across his upper body. His biceps bunched and rounded beneath the fabric as he grabbed his left thigh with both hands and lowered onto the couch.

"It might be better if you slip out of your jeans?" His scowl deepened, his lower lip curling up a little beneath the top one.

"Just do it over my pants again. Please."

She recalled the topography of dips and rises she'd felt through his jeans. The angles of his jaw were more pronounced as he clenched his teeth, a small muscle jumping in his cheek. Even in uncertainty and pain, Levi was the most breathtaking man she'd ever laid eyes on. Whatever his clothing hid, she'd accept it because it was a part of him. Her fingers tingled at the promise of soothing his pain, even as her heart geared up to protect itself.

"I stripped in front of you, buddy."

"No."

"Look, I use oil during therapy that helps the muscles relax. But you have to take your jeans off."

Levi's face was impassive, his fingers clenching even harder around his thigh. His shoulders softened a little, and just when she thought he might agree, he shifted as if to get up. Afraid that he was going to leave, Carrie crossed her arms and took a steadying breath. He couldn't leave—not in this much pain. She'd never rest knowing she'd let him walk out of here.

Time to pull out the big guns. "Are you scared?"

His eyes narrowed, his lips going thin. "What did you say?"

"You heard me, cowboy. Are you too scared to let me see, or are you man enough to let me help you?"

His chin came up and the steely expression was just what she'd hoped for. The marine in him wouldn't back down. Neither would the cowboy. "Don't give up on a challenge so fast, Levi. I'd be awfully disappointed."

His hand shot out and snagged her wrist, gently yanking her forward until her face was inches from his. A thrill raced through her, every inch of skin on her arms going electric. "I don't lose. Pants stay on. And by the way, Carrie Lynn, you seem to have forgotten how good I am at paybacks."

She huffed a short laugh. Hell no, she hadn't forgotten. It's what the wicked part of her—the one that still wanted him despite good sense—had been counting on.

• • •

He resisted the urge to get up and walk out because he needed the relief her hands could bring. Wary, but relenting, Levi lay back with one arm under his head and straightened his legs the best he could. It ate at him, lying vulnerable, and made it hard to stay still.

His lids wanted to drop, but no way was he taking his eyes off Carrie. Her hands moved carefully, purposefully, as she smoothed his jeans. At first, her firm touches were nearly unbearable. Forcing himself not to wince, Levi clenched his shoulders and took a tight breath. He'd been on horseback way too much today. Shit, not just today, this week in general. So much for taking it easy by fixing the fence.

"Breathe out, nice and long." Her soft voice had the same effect as a drill sergeant's yell, prompting him to do as he was told without question. Staring at the ceiling, he focused on even breathing, and slowly, the pain turned into an ache.

"Tell me what you've had done." She moved down past his knee, her palms soothingly warm through the denim. Levi's mouth was so dry he could barely speak.

"Hardware in my femur. Tendon surgery. Muscle debridement and grafting."

"Infection?"

"Oh yeah." Over half of his outer thigh muscle was gone, along with a good portion of the front. What hadn't been blown off had become infected, the disease leaving behind a network of ripped and sunken muscle. Lying in a hospital bed as long as he had allowed more muscle mass to waste away. When all was said and done, his thigh looked like a half-eaten drumstick. Tissue grafting had provided some extra padding and support. Therapy worked to strengthen the leg to support his body weight. Standing, walking, taking steps, driving, all became huge feats of willpower and perseverance.

Her touch went deeper, penetrating with the firm downward pressure. Levi groaned despite himself, instinctively leaning his head back.

Carrie started to speak, but stopped herself. Then, hesitantly, "Can you tell me about it? What happened to you?" Her hands were easing and pushing and prodding from his hip to his ankle and back up again. Though he knew she'd asked him something, Levi couldn't seem to pull himself together to answer. He was drifting too far into sensation. Forcing concentration, he briefly mulled over how much to say.

Whether it was the force of shock waves from the explosion that had damaged him so, or shrapnel, or both, he'd never found out. Never asked, because it wouldn't have changed anything. What was done was done. "Bomb."

"Were you in a vehicle? I've seen news reports on roadside bombs and how they'd hurt so many soldiers."

He winced as she hit a tender spot, but breathed through it. "No. I was climbing stairs…was supposed to check the upper level and hit a trip wire." Talking about that day brought back tension he'd tried so hard to get rid of. He'd never delved into memories of his last day as an active marine with anyone but his doctors, and the shrink he'd seen for a short time. Even with them, he'd kept the details mostly to himself, waving off the antidepressants they said would help with the anxiety and the shadows in his mind. Instead, he'd thrown himself into physical therapy and working out, and both had helped.

"Were you alone?"

He'd never been alone. Not when he slept, or ate, or had

a few minutes to read or listen to his iPod. And never on a mission.

"No." He dropped the word with unintentional venom, and he tried to feel sorry about that. Carrie let it go, and he was glad…figured he'd apologize later for being rude. Soon he was completely lost in the mix of pleasure and discomfort she was causing him. It was sensitive as hell, but the stabbing, life-altering pain was gone.

The scent of floral shampoo filled his senses as she bent near his side. Her strong fingers eased the knots and pins and needles from his flesh, eliciting a low moan he couldn't hold back. The warmth of her body seeped into his own.

"Better?" The low vibration of her voice brought tingles of pleasure over his limbs. He tried to answer but couldn't. Nodded instead.

"Shirt off and flip onto your belly."

That pulled him from the haze. Levi sat halfway. "What?"

She looked completely unfazed "Tension in your upper body can cause pain in other places. So, shirt off and flip."

Levi's cock twitched, surprising the hell out of him. Well, hello and thank you for deciding to pay attention now. At least lying on his stomach would hide the growing evidence of his thoughts. Levi reached across his body, pulling off his shirt. It wasn't graceful but he flipped, crossed his arms, and laid his forehead on top of them. Carrie's movements made soft sounds next to him. Every muscle in his back tensed in anticipation of what she might do next. He couldn't see, but he could imagine.

She'd rub oil between her palms and put her warmed hands on his shoulders. Her fingers would dig into the straps of muscle over his back and knead with just enough pressure to make him hold his breath. She'd lean down close enough that her shirt would tickle his skin, her breasts hovering just above his back as she leaned into the massage…

Levi mumbled a quiet curse to get his thoughts under control. Silence filled the room. Turning his head slightly, Levi peeked. Carrie stood next to him, her hands frozen in front of her, eyes trained on his back. His brow fell, his brain running through his catalog of injuries. Nope, nothing back there he'd forgotten to tell her about.

"Something wrong?"

She licked her lips and looked a little dazed. "You're just so damn beautiful." Carrie's eyes went round, her mouth dropping open. "I...I mean—"

Shit, his cock was completely awake now, pressing painfully into the soft cushions. He pushed up on his elbows, his brain absorbing her words.

"Down!" She nudged him back into place and he allowed it, but not before he'd seen the blush on her cheeks. Smiling, he was glad to bury his face in his crossed arms to give them some space. She was giving him an endorphin high with this massage stuff, and her words, her closeness, were driving his libido through the ever-loving roof.

Her hands began to work his shoulder muscles, massaging and digging and smoothing along his neck, his back, the curve of his waist. Time sloughed off as he sank into...something...a daydream state, maybe? His body seemed to sway as if he were floating, but instead of being in water, he found himself standing in the desert, looking at a singular row of buildings. His friend Carlos adjusted his night vision goggles and made a sweep with his hand as if Levi should follow.

No one was supposed to go inside—at least, that was the feeling going through him. Going in was wrong. Bad. Unsafe. He tried to tell Carlos to wait, but his friend was already going up the long, black metal staircase on the side of the building. One step. Two...five. Levi followed, tried to reach out and grab Carlos's shirt to tug him back down, but he was too far ahead.

Carlos turned with a huge, toothy smile, his Hispanic accent thick and way too cheerful for the circumstances. "'Bout damn time you caught up, cowboy."

"Wait!" He grabbed for Carlos, but no one was there. Just inky darkness punched with tiny little stars.

"Did that hurt?" Someone was tapping on him. He turned his head, groggy yet perfectly clear. The shadows in his mind disappeared like a fog, leaving behind the bitter aftertaste that always followed when he remembered that day. It was over—he was safe, alive, with the only woman he'd ever imagined coming home to standing right here.

Levi made a half flip, reaching for her. Carrie's brow was furrowed, her touch gentle as she threaded her fingers through his.

"Better?" Carrie touched his cheek, the soft imprint of her fingertips grounding him to the here and now. Confusion bled into clarity, remnants of the dream skipping off as desire, hot and demanding, replaced it. Levi snagged the back of her neck with one hand and pulled her down to him.

Her lips met his with a cascade of sweetness. Her mouth parted, urging him in deeper, wider, her tongue meeting his in a hot slide. His hands wound up in her soft curls, pulling her closer until he was completely lost in her warm, wet mouth and the pleasure of her lips on his.

He pulled back just a little to trace her lower lip with his tongue before nipping it gently with his teeth. One of her hands gripped the back of his neck, her other raking into his hair, the pads of her fingers drawing shocks over his scalp. The moan she let loose was so fucking satisfying, Levi's chest welled and clenched, his groin tugging with a deep ache.

"Payback time," he whispered, trailing his right hand down her neck, over her back where he cupped between her shoulder blades and held her tight. She followed him in, bringing an openmouthed kiss closed, and leaned into the quick little kisses he pressed against her mouth. She sucked his lower lip between hers before she pulled back and leaned her cheek against his and whispered, "I don't know what to do with you."

Levi leaned back, making her look at him. "What do you mean?"

"We can't do this." She pulled away from him. "I want to know you again. I want to be part of your life, but it can't be like this." Levi sat and swung his legs over the side of the couch and stood easily. He'd already told himself the same thing this morning, but here he was kissing her again. Thing was, he could give a damn about what he'd decided this morning. It didn't feel right, deep in that place inside that he'd come to listen to. Holding her, keeping her close, being here with her. That felt right.

That's what flooded him with peace and contentment.

"Why?" A simple question, but it mattered so much. He fixed things, solved problems. Whatever the obstacle, they'd find a way. He'd been told he'd probably never walk again without crutches, but here he was on his own two feet. He could lift her up, too, if she'd just open up to him.

"Just friends, Levi."

"You've thought about more." He wanted to touch her, use his hands and his lips to convince her that they could definitely have more. "You have, haven't you?"

"Of course I have. I loved you once!" Her voice broke. "But I have my future to think about and I don't see this ending well for us."

She was scared. He'd never downplay that. Hell, he was scared, too. Mostly about making the wrong choices when it came to her…moving too fast, moving too slow. Not weighing the options. Putting her in harm's way. Letting her go without a fight.

Spotting his jacket on a chair, he walked over to retrieve

it. For now, he'd back off, give her space. But he wasn't done trying to pull this thing between them together.

"Just friends?" He put his coat on, amazed at how fluid his legs felt. She gave a short nod, less than convincing, but he'd let it go. They walked back into the kitchen and crossed to the door.

"Levi?" The screen shut, separating them. "Friends don't kiss. Not like that."

He pushed the door open and crossed the threshold, giving her a wink as he looked back. "No more kissing?"

"I mean it."

The scent of citrus and flowers wafted off his coat from when she'd been wearing it this morning. Shoving his hands in his pockets, Levi descended the steps. "We'll see, Carrie Lynn. We'll see."

Chapter Eleven

Wiping sweat from her forehead on the crook of her arm, Carrie was grateful for the breeze blowing in through the open barn doors. It was balmy today, a rare warm spell in a month that usually brought chilly air and rain. She'd sent her dad off to Colorado with a hug and a stock trailer full of prime cattle, in the hue of early morning that promised to be a beautiful day.

When she was a teenager, he'd been reluctant to leave her overnight alone in case her blood sugar plummeted. Several times, he'd found her unconscious on the floor. There wasn't an ambulance in Greenbrook, so he'd give her a shot her doctor had prescribed for emergencies to get her blood sugar up, and drive her forty-five minutes to the closest hospital. Sometimes, it was a cycle of rinse and repeat.

Other times, like now, her sugars would be great and she'd go months without a hypoglycemic episode. It was going on a year now since she'd had a debilitating low. She wasn't worried about her dad being gone, or about being mostly alone while he was. The ranch hands were around, some of them living on-site in the bunkhouse. And the Haywoods would be stopping by. Despite being rain-soaked and cold yesterday, she felt fine.

If she had to name a problem, it would be Levi.

He'd always had to slip the last word into any argument. Typical man, all, "We'll see, Carrie Lynn. We'll see." No, they would not see. Steadying herself on the ladder, Carrie pulled thick leather gloves from her back pocket and put them on. She'd noticed four broken windows in the horse barn the other day, the two-foot wide rectangular ones that topped each stall. Before they could be changed, the remaining shards of glass needed to be broken out.

She'd already taken care of two windows, finding deep satisfaction each time she tapped the glass pieces and watched them fall outside, landing onto the tarps she'd laid on the ground to catch the debris.

Too bad she couldn't turn her problems into glass and destroy each one. Bad vision? *Crash*. Boredom with life in general? *Crack*. Unresolved feelings for Levi that got worse each time he kissed her? Smash, shatter, destroy.

She tapped a large piece out of the window frame with her hammer, wishing she could obliterate it. She had to be careful that each chunk fell onto the tarp, so Hulk-smashing was out of the question, sadly. The next piece was smaller and she hit it with enough force to crack it in two before it fell.

"Huh," she muttered, peeking carefully through the frame to be sure the glass landed on the tarp. "That felt good."

"Trying to turn it back into sand?"

Carrie wobbled on the ladder, recognizing the voice with a groan.

"Something like that." She didn't bother to look at him. He'd be dead sexy and she didn't need that right now. Yesterday had thrown her into Levi overload and she was still buzzing inside.

"Why don't you come on down?"

She rolled her eyes. He probably had both gloved hands on his lean hips, one leg cocked in that way he had to let everyone know he was the shit. And if she didn't obey him, he'd look at the ground and tell her again, waiting for her to listen on her own accord before he had to press the issue. Oh, Levi, she thought. He'd always been stubborn and bossy and hot as sin.

"I'm good."

A pause. She had to look, just to see. Sure enough, his hands were on his hips.

"Carrie, come down."

"Don't you have something to do?" God, she was so tired of people telling her what she could and couldn't do. Always making decisions for her instead of with her, even now, when she was a grown woman. Even in Wyoming, her aunts were constantly fussing as if she were a fragile little thing. She hadn't told anyone about her vision for a reason. Being henpecked and waited on hand and foot didn't sound that appealing.

She tapped at tiny chunks of glass around the frame, scooping them into her gloved palm and letting them drop. A deep, frustrated sigh below her...she counted to three...and the ladder trembled as if he'd gripped it.

"Get down. You're going to get hurt."

"I'll take my chances."

She heard shuffling from the ground, and she figured he was going to come up, and what, pull her down? "Before you go all caveman on me, Levi, I have a question." She paused with the hammer in midair, realizing what she was about to ask him. Her pulse ticked up. Was she really going to go there? The truth would come spilling out, and he'd know.

He'd know.

"Yeah?"

"How'd you do it?" She made a half turn, hanging on to the ladder sides to look down at him. Beautiful, just as she'd suspected, with his black hair glinting in the light, his broad shoulders covered in blue-and-white flannel. "When you were lying in the hospital, and you knew your body was changed and wouldn't be the same…how did you get better?"

His hands relaxed their grip. A long pause worried her that he wasn't going to answer, but then he shrugged. "Some days, I'm still not better, Carrie." Tapping a finger to his head, he took a step back. "That day that changed my body? One of my best friends was killed and I carry that up here, locked away. I knew I could be stubborn enough to walk again. But my mind? That was the biggest obstacle. I didn't know how to handle the depression that followed."

He'd been through so much, more than anyone would ever know, really. Looking at him now, strong and healthy, she was awed that he'd made it through when so many in a similar situation might not. If anyone could help her acclimate to losing her sight, it was him.

"When you realized, that first time, that your legs were damaged—" She stopped herself, not really sure how to phrase her question. "When you knew, without a doubt, that you were physically altered, how did you come to accept it?"

His face softened. "Carrie." His voice was soft and tender. "What's this about?"

She turned back to the window, though there wasn't any more glass to smash. A part of her wanted to brush the matter off and forget it. But now that he'd opened up a little, she was hungry for more, to know him and that huge part of his life that she'd missed. Maybe she wanted him to know her, too.

"Come down here and talk to me."

Maintaining some distance gave her confidence that she could go through with this conversation. If he touched her, she might break down completely. "I'm not done up here."

Another sigh and then the sound of rustling hay. He'd grabbed a rake and was cleaning bedding on the stall floor. "Truthfully, after the doctors let me out of the medical coma, I didn't care if I lived or died."

Carrie clenched her eyes at the hint of pain in his tone.

"I'd look down and see what was left of my legs and rage inside. I was pissed that I'd be that way the rest of my life. I came home to Paint River and watched my brothers and my new sisters-in-law go about their lives—working, riding, driving—and I realized…"

His voice trailed away, along with the sound of the rake. The back of her neck tingling, Carrie set down the hammer on the window frame. "Realized what?"

"That Paint River's dirt had my sweat and blood in it. My feet had walked that land since I first learned how, and damn it, I wanted to walk it again." Rake tines scraped the rubber floor. "I figured, changed or not, it was either live and be alive, or be alive but not live. So here I am, hundreds of physical therapy hours and lots of fear later, alive and living."

Staring out the open window, she tracked the sway of a tree across the yard as his words hit her heart. She hadn't done very much living since getting the news that her sight was changing.

"First thing you've got to do, though, is have a raging fit about it."

"What?"

"A fit. You know, scream, yell, and smash things…like windows." He set the rake aside and took a purposeful step to the ladder. In a blink, he was climbing up behind her, face determined, sultry eyes locked on hers. Unable to drum up a protest, she gripped the sides tighter as the ladder trembled with his climb. Two rungs below her, his body heat spread over the backs of her legs. He slid a hand up her right hip to the curve of her waist, his fingers giving a light tug on her shirt.

"Talk to me. Come down." He urged her to come down one step and she complied, little quakes rumbling through her at his proximity. "One more." Her body pressed against his as she descended one more rung, his arms bracing on either side of her. The brush of his shirt against her back lit goose bumps along her arms. She turned as much as she could, desperate to see what was in his eyes.

His face was so close to hers...just close enough that if she leaned down a tiny bit, she could...

"You said no more kissing."

With a sharp intake of breath, Carrie realized her lips were nearly touching his. She was being a total hypocrite, but she couldn't make herself move away. "I did say that."

"Did you mean it?"

Thankfully the rung was too narrow for her to turn or face him. Otherwise she'd do so and press against him, encourage his hands to slide up her sides. "I want to mean it."

Levi grinned and she did, too, leaning in a little more because she really didn't know if she meant it or not. Another little taste, just to see...

"Uncle Levi!"

Levi pulled back abruptly, his grip on either side of her keeping Carrie from startling right off the ladder. Cole's daughter, Birdie, waved as she bounced down the aisle, Sophie Haywood behind her. A slow expression of amusement and suspicion crossed Sophie's face as she stopped outside the stall.

"We tried the house, but no one answered, so figured we'd try in here."

Birdie gripped her aunt's hand and peered up at them with big, shy eyes. Clearing his throat, Levi climbed down and held the ladder as she did the same.

"So, Carrie," Sophie said with a side-eye look at Levi. "Rylan and I got free spa day passes thanks to Levi here impressing one of the candidates." She nudged him with her elbow. "Remember the one who smeared you in chocolate? Yeah, her. She says hello, by the way."

He gave Sophie an impatient look before walking away, pausing to ruffle Birdie's hair.

"We'll finish this conversation later, Carrie." He disappeared, leaving her to bear Sophie's knowing grin alone.

"Anyway, do you want to come with?"

"Yes. When?" A spa day with women she hoped to know better? Heck, yeah.

Sophie put an arm around her shoulders. "Now."

Chapter Twelve

A week ago, his life had been pretty uncomplicated. Get up, work, eat, go to bed, repeat. Since Carrie had shown up, his days had become riddled with constant wondering. Something was off with her. He'd sensed it when they got caught in the storm, but he'd brushed it off. She rubbed her eyes a lot and seemed more interested in slipping into deep thought than talking. They'd spent years apart; he didn't know her like he once had. Maybe that's all it was. He expected her to be the same chatty, vivacious Carrie he'd left behind.

Her questions in the barn this morning nailed his concern. This was more than a personality change brought on by time and maturity. Something was up with her, and it left an ominous feeling in his gut.

Instead of focusing on making plans for Agate Falls, as he should be doing, he was wrapped up in mulling over conversations he needed to have, and a bunch of nagging questions that he needed to ask. All these loose ends frustrated him and it was time to tie everything up before he lost his mind.

Finishing up at Agate Falls, he went into Greenbrook to the hardware store, and then drove home to Paint River with the radio cranked, trying to get Carrie out of his head. That didn't last too long when he pulled up to the ranch house to find her truck parked out front.

Sweaty, hungry, and wondering what she was up to, Levi walked into the house and paused.

His brothers and Jaxon were kicked back at the kitchen table, Cole with one boot braced on the side of the table as he saluted Levi with a beer bottle. That no-good, cut-the-tail-off-the-dog grin he wore meant trouble.

"Hey there, little brother. 'Bout time you showed up."

"What's up, boys?" Levi ran a hand over his face, not liking Tucker's self-satisfied smirk.

Cole pulled out a chair beside him and gave it a hearty pat. "Have a seat. I hope you have your marine corps panties on."

Levi begrudgingly sat. Tucker flicked the toothpick in his mouth and pulled a bottle of whiskey from behind his back and set it on the table. "Seems our wives have taken Carrie Lynn to Missoula to enjoy an all-expenses-paid trip to the day spa."

Sophie had mentioned that this morning. Seemed the women didn't waste any time taking up the offer for free pampering.

Cole slid a quart-sized mason jar next to the whiskey. "They dropped Birdie off with Aunt Penny until tomorrow, and Ma and Jim are at Glacier National so we're going to settle up the Haywood way."

Levi eyed the mason jar like it contained live snakes. Actually, snakes would be better.

He groaned. "Oh, hell no." The clear liquid inside the jar revealed neatly stacked green jalapeños, red tabasco peppers, whole garlic cloves, and yellow habanero peppers, surrounded by brown dill heads.

"We saved a jar of Ma's ball burners just for you, buddy." Cole cracked the ring on the jar, popped the sealed top. "You know the routine." A shot glass appeared in front of him. Levi leaned back in the chair and spread his knees wide, a hand on his middle. His ma made the "ball burners" to use for the chili-eating contest at the Greenbrook Fair every year. To date, no one had been able to finish an entire bowl, and she had more ribbons than a duck did feathers.

And goddammit, this game was no joke. He'd been twenty the first time they'd played, and it had been three in the afternoon the next day before any of them could peel themselves off the basement floor.

"I coughed up blood for two days the last time we did this," he groaned. A quarter slid across the table and came to rest beside Levi's shot glass.

"You take any fancy pain pills today?" Cole asked.

"Hell no." Levi grimaced as a waft of garlic and vinegar hit his nose.

"Well, I'd say your chance of dying is reduced by a couple percentage points then."

"What are we settling up about?"

Tucker pulled the toothpick from his mouth and cracked open the whiskey. "We have too much work and not enough of us, so we're drinking for it. Loser gets to handle the charity in California that wants to put a therapeutic riding center here."

Levi scoffed. "Look, I've been meaning to tell you guys but we didn't have the time to sit down like this. I bought in on Agate Falls." Silence fell. He looked to each man and spread his hands wide. "I've got my hands full, but—"

"You're shittin' me." Cole sat forward in his chair. "When did this happen?"

"Three weeks or so."

Cole tapped his empty shot glass on the table, and Tucker filled it up, made his way around until everyone's glass was full. "Cheers, Levi."

Levi lifted his glass high as they did the same and then tossed back the liquor. The whiskey streaked fire down his throat. He stifled a cough. It was only the beginning and he was already regretting it. He swallowed hard.

"I'm still here for you guys." He'd put this conversation off partly because he'd been afraid his brothers would be resentful of the lack of time he'd now have for Paint River things. Instead, they looked slightly impressed, and way more interested in refilling their shot glasses than continuing this conversation.

"Good, then you get the therapy center project." Tucker leaned across the table and refilled Levi's glass.

"Hell no. You said we're drinking for it, so we're drinking for it."

Tucker scooted his chair slightly sideways and rested an arm on the table. "Quarter."

Levi leaned forward. "I hate to break it to you assholes, but you'll be the only ones eating those peppers if we play straight quarters. There wasn't much else to do to pass the nights in Afghanistan. I've got this in the bag." Levi picked up the coin and bounced it off the table and straight into the shot glass. It swirled twice before clunking to the bottom. Tucker shot to his feet with challenge on his face.

"Oh yeah, show-off?" He disappeared into the kitchen, came back with an armful of glasses. He set a tall glass in the middle and arranged five smaller glasses around it. When he was done, each cup contained a shot of whiskey, and either a garlic clove or a slice of pepper. The middle had a double shot and a fat jalapeño slice. Levi laughed and shook his head as Tucker slid him the quarter.

"Doesn't matter how many times you score, you're still

drinking or eating something. Oh, and if you miss, you take a bite of the Mother." Tucker stabbed a fork into the middle of the jar, withdrawing the meanest-looking habanero Levi had ever seen.

"Speaking of mother," Cole said before he drained his glass. "She asked that you personally take on the project. So just do it."

Levi folded his hands over his stomach. "Nice try."

Cole set his glass down with flair, indicating that Jaxon should fill it up. "You're not going to let her down, are you?"

Levi sucked in a breath through his nose and smirked at Cole. If his ma had wanted him to take on the project, she'd have come right out and asked. He sensed a deeper reason for this impromptu let's-get-sloshed party, like maybe the fact that the four of them had spent little time together that didn't involve work. Cole had a new baby coming. Tucker had a new wife and Jaxon worked sunup to sundown, barely showing the whites of his eyes until well after dark.

So fine, he'd sit here and drink with them, and humor them in the process. Raising his glass, he gave a nod. "Here's to not letting Ma down."

The better part of three hours passed and Levi couldn't figure out what the hell happened to his chair. The damn thing wouldn't stop swaying.

"Goddammit." Levi's lips and tongue were puffy as if they'd been inflated and smashed onto his face. He put his fingers there, surprised they didn't feel bigger when he touched them. The Mother sat next to the empty whiskey bottle, still impaled with a fork and remarkably smaller in size. His gut rumbled and clenched, reminding him where the pieces of Mother had gone. The table looked slightly crooked, like a leg had buckled and pitched the top sideways. Levi blinked, cocked his head.

"Sit up. You can't...drink like that." Something nudged

him hard in the biceps. Levi's head snapped up, and he realized he'd been resting his head on the table. The slide of a quarter and the cool feel of metal against his fingertips. Levi looked from Cole to Tucker and Jaxon. They were swirling, making it impossible to focus. He ran a hand over his eyes, confused for a moment.

The table used to be full of more men, crowded so tightly around that you couldn't discern one face from the other. White T-shirts, tan desert camo pants, dog tags shining in the overhead light. Clinking, laughing, talking—the drone would get so loud that you couldn't make out a single word. Cards flipping, cans crushing in animated hands, fists pounding on the plastic tabletop so hard the whole thing shook.

Lights would flicker, and the faces would become encased in shadows. Silence would fall if the lights stayed off too long, the soldiers listening for the sirens…for the call. But then a white fluorescent glow would burst through the room, and the voices and cards picked up where they left off. Once, the lights didn't go back on, and the ground shook like a sinkhole was going to rip open and swallow them down. The next thing he knew, he was following Carlos out into the night… driving…thinking about Carrie and if he'd ever see her again.

Levi looked around, his palms on the table to keep his ass steady in the chair. Jaxon made a face at him, grounding him in the present. Even then, he'd been thinking about Carrie. Shit.

"Damn boy, you look sick. Is The Mother making little pepper babies in your belly?" Jaxon snorted. Tucker slapped the table as they laughed. "Man, it's good to have you home, Levi. I missed picking on you."

Levi's fingers dug into his sweaty palms, making tight fists, the movement helping him focus on not falling backward.

"Remember that time you made Levi eat the—"

"We aren't here to act like women." Levi looked up. His

head was swimming, spinning, making it hard for him to hold it up. "Keep your sappy estrogen-talk to yourself."

Tucker tried to scratch his forehead and knocked his hat off. "You dumbass. If we…if we were going to girl-talk, we'd be talking about Carrie." He produced a full bottle from under the table and cracked the top, refilled everyone's glass. Levi put his forearms on the table to hold himself up.

"What about her?"

Tucker took his shot and followed it with a loud shout before he slammed the glass down. "You're hard for her, man. We all know why you *really* grabbed Agate Falls."

He flipped Tucker the finger. "Shut up, Tuck."

His middle brother didn't know when to quit, never had, especially when the booze ran freely. "She still loves you." The words came out in a sloppy singsong that sounded a lot like a taunt. What the hell was this, high school? Levi gave a disgusted shake of his head. She didn't love him, far from it. *I loved you once.*

"No, she doesn't."

Cole gave him an exaggerated pat on the knee. "Don't worry, man. *We* love you."

"Speak for yourself." Tucker hiccuped around a grin.

"Shut up, Tuck." The slurred amusement in Cole's voice pulled Levi from the empty pit his brain seemed to be in. He snickered and rubbed his blurry eyes with one hand. Mostly quiet this entire time, Jaxon leaned across the table, startling Levi a little with the sound of his voice. "When're you gonna tell her that you want her to stay?"

When did these three idiots become relationship experts? They hadn't even been in the same place long enough for any of them to get a good read on what was going on with him and Carrie. Unless…he was really that obvious.

"I don't love Carrie." Whoa, did that feel wrong spouting out between his crazy puffy-feeling lips.

Both brothers laughed. "Right." Tucker kicked back his chair, slouched down and stretched out his long legs. "Sooner you admit it…sooner you can get that girl in bed."

Levi grabbed Cole's shot glass and downed the whiskey with a sudden thought of naked Carrie. Sleek, smooth, long-legged, naked Carrie. He'd already had her in bed, a long time ago. Calling his name as he made her come. And then he'd walked away. He couldn't ask her to go with him, not when it meant taking her away from the security of her family, and not after the promise he'd made Darren.

"Wrong. I think she hates me a little."

Tucker snorted. "You stupid son of a—"

Levi grabbed the edge of the table to keep from falling off the top of the world. This. Damn. Chair. "Your wife let you…talk like that?" That was it, he was falling. He tipped, his fingers losing their grip.

"She don't…*let* me do…anything." Tucker wagged a hand at him—maybe it was just a finger—no way to tell because his eyes were closing.

Levi made a last-ditch attempt to stay upright. He glanced past Tucker. Damn, it looked like Sophie standing there… and Rylan. And then a head of curly blond hair peeked in between the two women.

Oh shit, there's Carrie Lynn. And he went for the floor.

Chapter Thirteen

"Well, this is unexpected."

Carrie stood next to Rylan, whose arms were crossed over her pregnant belly. Cole and Levi tipped toward each other, neither of them actually making it to the floor. Instead, they made an awkward pyramid with their shoulders butted and their heads pressed together. Tucker was slumped in the chair, head thrown back, apparently out cold.

She'd had a great time in Missoula at the spa. Hair, nails, skin, all shiny and refreshed. Carrie was still tingly inside that the girls had asked her to come along, seeing how they didn't really know her that well. Growing up here, she'd been the only girl and had gotten used to hanging around adolescent boys real fast. Even now, she found she related to men more than women, but Sophie and Rylan had made her feel completely welcome. She had half a mind to go home and enjoy the afterglow, and let Levi steep in his own intoxication.

The dining room table was littered with empty whiskey bottles, glasses, spilled liquor and…peppers. Carrie eyed the vegetables, many stabbed with forks and half eaten, the smell nearly singeing her nose.

"Yikes." She pulled back from the strong, spicy odor.

Rylan heaved a sigh. "I can't believe they mixed Maeve's peppers with whiskey. There will be so much pain tomorrow."

Sophie nodded, hands on her hips, with a grin that implied she wouldn't mind kicking her husband out of bed and hearing him *thunk* onto the floor. Carrie swept a gaze over Levi. The sight of him leaning like a fallen tree against his equally drunk brother was stupidly funny. All it would take was for one of them to shift or twitch, and they'd both go crashing down.

"Better wake them up," Carrie suggested. "Cold water will do it." It only took a minute for the other women to return with full glasses. Carrie put a hand on Levi's shoulder, trying to see his face behind his mop of curls. She put another hand on Cole and stepped back. "Go for it."

The water came down; the men roared to life. Levi's arms came out on either side of his body, his fingers making a fist in Carrie's shirt. He jerked back in the chair, pulling Carrie forward so she launched onto his lap.

She gasped, her hands clutching his hips to brace herself. Behind her, Cole made a fuss as Rylan helped him up. A chair crashed. Sophie swore like a sailor. Jaxon blubbered apologies. The bewildered look on Levi's face, combined with the water dripping off his curls onto her forearms and the ruckus behind her, made laughter well up inside. It bubbled up in her chest, escaped her lips. Her head dipped on its own accord, bringing the top of her forehead against his abdomen. A hand slid into her hair. Her breath stalled, the memory of their kiss flashing through her mind.

"No more kissing," Levi mumbled as his eyes closed.

Carrie scrambled off him and socked him in the shoulder. "Come on. To the couch." Having no idea just how unsteady he might be, she eyeballed the open space between dining and living room and figured there was enough furniture for him to hang on to make it that far.

Levi stood much faster and steadier than she'd have thought. Her hands went palm-out against his chest. "Geez, slow down." The smooth, tanned skin of his forehead bunched into deep lines as he made his way to the living room. He was nearly there when he stopped, reached across his body with his left hand and pulled his shirt off. "Hot in here."

"Oh crap." Carrie sucked in a slow breath. Levi, Levi, Levi. All that rock-solid male flesh that she'd been dreaming about. It never failed, the moment her head hit the pillow, his half-naked body came to mind. It was a small wonder she hadn't exploded from lack of sleep and rampant sexual frustration. Damn him.

"You got this, Carrie?" Sophie called from the front door. Tucker's arm was around her shoulder, as if that small woman could hold up a man his size. Yet somehow, she was doing it. Rylan had a fistful of Cole's shirt in her hand and was dragging him along. "If I go into labor tonight, I'm cutting your balls off with a razor blade."

Levi rounded the couch, the squeak and slide of skin on leather marking his body weight as he flopped down onto the cushions. She was throwing a blanket on top of him and going home. "I got it. Thanks again for the fun day." She waved the foursome and Jaxon out the door, realizing a moment later that it was just her and a very drunk, already-snoring Levi. A very tempting-even-though-he's-wasted Levi.

His left hand flopped off the couch and waved in her direction. She moved toward him and his fingers slid over the side of her knee. Her breath hitched.

"Carrie…stay."

Wow, drunk and delusional. She grabbed a throw pillow, thought about whacking him across the head with it. "I'm not staying." No matter how tempting he looked, all sprawled out like this. His scruffy face relaxed, the lines around his forehead and eyes almost nonexistent. She lifted his head and stuffed the pillow under him. Curls flopped over his brow and she softly brushed them back, letting her fingers linger in the silkiness of his hair. It was nice to touch him, comforting, sweetly familiar.

"What if I get cold?" His voice was small, sleepy and so unlike him that she couldn't help but laugh. She'd never seen him like this.

"You have a blanket right here."

"What if I fall off the couch?"

"Serves you right." She moved to the side table and flicked on the lamp.

His arm crossed across his chest. "What if I need you?"

"Why would you need me?"

When he didn't answer, she thought he'd drifted off, which would be great so she could grab her bag and slip out of here…

"I never stopped needing you." The words were followed by a low snore, his breathing going heavy and deep. That he'd essentially passed out didn't take away the shock of what he'd said. Words jumbled by alcohol, that's all. Or was it possible that he'd really kept her in his heart all this time? It seemed unlikely that he would, after he'd left her without advance notice and walked away from their love like it had meant nothing. It still stung as if the wound was fresh, and his confession, drunk or not, pulled apart what had healed.

Unfolding the blanket at his feet, she covered him with it, letting her gaze linger on his peaceful face. He'd opened up to her quite a bit this morning in the barn, sharing his personal hell with her. Letting her in. It was useless to deny that they still had a connection, and that maybe she'd pushed a bit to see if it was still there. It was, at least for her, and maybe the booze helped Levi realize it was there for him, too.

She didn't hate him. The opposite was starting to be true, no matter how she wanted to deny it.

A *boom* sounded over the house, jerking her attention to the window. Hurrying to the sliding doors that led to the porch, she was met with splashes of rain hitting the glass. The storm that had threatened all day had finally decided to let loose. Screw the wet season. All this rain made it hard for her to see while driving. Add the complete darkness outside and she was grounded.

"Shit," she huffed. Looking over her shoulder to where Levi lay on the couch, she weighed risking the short drive home versus staying until the storm passed. It was coming down steadier by the second. She'd be soaked by the time she ran down to her truck, and with her sight so limited, ending up in the ditch while it stormed wasn't a great alternative.

With an irritated groan, she wandered back to the couch, spying a perfect spot on the soft leather where Levi had curled up his legs. Another throw pillow sat there, looking all poufy and cozy after her long day. She plopped down on the cushion, back stiff as she measured whether Levi would stay asleep. When he didn't rouse, she curled into the space.

His even breathing mixed with the raindrops outside, creating a cozy melody that should have helped her relax, but didn't. Well aware of the close proximity of his body, Carrie closed her eyes as a memory weaseled in—Levi lying on his side on a woven blanket in the hay, propped on one elbow, looking down at her while he absently twirled a piece of hay between his lips. She'd been on the fence rail, watching him and Tucker work a new horse, when Levi had jumped off, handed the reins to his brother, and come her way. Without a word, he'd slipped through the rails and nodded for her to follow him. She had, and they'd barely stepped into the horse barn when his hands gripped her waist and he pulled her into a stall.

"I've been crushing on you long enough, Carrie Lynn.

You gonna be mine, yes or no?" And then he'd kissed her with the gusto of a fifteen-year-old, and they'd fallen into the hay. It had been the moment she felt certain that this boy she'd known forever was going to be something more. He had a deeply rooted meaning in her life that would grow and likely change with time, but would never wither away completely. It was as true now as it had been then.

Sinking into the memory, she was lulled by the rain on the roof. A loud groan startled her. Disoriented, Carrie sat up, realizing she must have drifted off. Levi sat on the edge of the couch.

"My *head*."

His arms moved slowly as he rubbed his hands over his face with another groan. She eyed the smooth, sexy slide of his muscles as he moved and the way his tan skin shone in the soft, golden lamplight. Panty incineration starts in ten, nine, eight... Carrie rolled her eyes. *Knock it off!*

"No kidding, genius. Whose idea was that little drinking party, anyway?"

He blew out a breath and rested his elbows on his knees. "Not mine. Hey, who passed out last?" He straightened, looking at her expectantly like it was the most important question in the history of mankind.

"Uh, you did?"

"Thank God!" Wincing, he grabbed his head between his hands. "Ouch."

Carrie shook her head and yawned. The clock above the fireplace showed 2:00 a.m., and she was feeling it. Standing, she crossed to peek out the patio doors, frowning to see the rain hadn't let up at all behind the glow of the porch lights. As soon as it did, she was out of here.

"I'll be right back," Levi said, the couch squeaking as he rose. A burst of thunder went over the house, followed by the flicker of lights. Glancing around, she expected the power to go out and hoped it wouldn't. She'd never been afraid of the dark until faced with the possibility that she might eventually live in a lightless world.

Weary, she turned back toward the living room, resigned to sink into the couch and wait out the storm. Halfway there, thunder boomed again, taking the power with it as she'd feared, throwing the room into soulless dark. Hugging herself, she stood rooted in place, waiting to see if the lights would come back.

This is silly, she thought, trying to shake herself out of the inane fear. Six months ago, she'd walk through the house in the pitch black, wasn't afraid to go out into the night. Why did that have to change, especially so rapidly? It seemed she could barely get a grip on one thing before another piece fell away.

"Carrie?" Levi's voice came from the hall, filling her with relief. "Where are you?"

"Here." Nonspecific, but the best she could manage. Footfalls came near, the scent of soap and mint preceding his uncertain touch on her arm. "Hey, you're trembling." Was she?

"Don't tell me the girl who used to watch horror movies without lights on is scared of the dark." His quip didn't make her feel any better, but his nearness did. When his thumb began a soft back-and-forth over her wrist, she leaned into him.

"I'm fine." Blinking hard, she hoped to see some stream of light cut through the room. Even if the moon were out, it would be shrouded by the storm. His hand grappled for hers, finding it and threading their fingers together. Leading her until her leg bumped the side of the couch, Levi sank down and pulled her gently with him. She sat, feeling around her to find his hip next to hers. Only when she touched his thigh did she realize how cold her fingers were, how much her body shook.

"When I was in the desert and it was black as Ma's coffee, I'd look up and wish the stars to come out to give us some light.

Mostly, it stayed dark and we had to punch down our nerves and make it through." A soft touch on her hair, and then the stroke of fingers through the strands. The strain in his tone was the same he'd had when telling her about his injuries this morning. "Truth? I couldn't watch a horror movie in the dark now if you paid me." The pleasure of his caress spread over her entire scalp as he stroked her hair. "What changed for you, Carrie?"

It was a simple, valid question. He'd likely homed in on something going on with her after the questions she'd asked him in the barn this morning. Funny how she'd become adept at hiding her disability from everyone, but with Levi, her body was giving it away.

Levi had been open with her about his war experience. She'd told no one about herself, always making excuses for the times her vision made her stumble or restricted her in some way. Voicing it, hearing the words from her own lips, would cement the prognosis. She couldn't tell him. Not yet.

"What if the dark never goes away?"

He pulled her down in one steady move. Her forearms went against his chest as both his hands found her hair, kneading her temples and sending her into a delicious haze. "You make your own light." A warm kiss on her forehead made her catch her breath. "Hey, you're safe and I'm here for you, *with* you." His lips cruised her face, gently, lovingly, punching a sob in her throat. "Do you understand, Sunshine? You're not alone."

His arms went around her and Carrie settled into his chest, the thud of his heart beneath her cheek. She wasn't alone. She knew that. There were a lot of people in her life that would be supportive when she told them her truth. She lightly gripped his shirt, hanging on to this moment in case it passed and never brought another like it. The only person she wanted with her was here, working his way back into her life. And her heart.

Chapter Fourteen

"Wake up, Sleeping Ugly."

Levi woke with a start as something slapped his stomach. Cole stood next to him like a hungover vulture—stubbled jaw, heavily lidded eyes, and a frown that could scare the devil.

Years of practice in the military had given Levi the ability to wake up alert at a second's notice. He made his voice high-pitched and squeaky. "Good morning, sweetheart."

Cole grimaced and pressed three fingers to his temple. "Not funny."

Seemed his brother was the worst of the two of them. Smug, Levi sat up, regretting it immediately as his head pressurized. A large manila envelope crinkled on his lap as he moved. "What's this?"

Cole huffed. "Your latest project."

The return address was from some therapy center in California. Pulling out a sheet of paper, he frowned at the heading, *New Abilities Therapeutic Riding Center.* Oh, hell no. He shoved the paper back inside and handed it to his brother. "I didn't lose. Carrie said I was the last one awake."

He frowned and glanced at the clock, realizing it was almost ten in the morning. Carrie was gone. Had she even been there last night or had it been a whiskey-soaked illusion?

"She's biased." Cole flopped the envelope onto the couch. "Just read the proposal and let me know what you think."

Standing, Levi strode past his brother toward the hall. Shower, then coffee. Lots of it, so he could sort through last night. Probably his imagination, but he thought he caught a whiff of Carrie's shampoo coming from his shirt. "I'll add it to the bottom of my to-do pile." He pulled on the fabric and sniffed. Well, dang. Strawberries.

"Look," Cole grouched. "She's going to be gone soon. You'll need work to drown in until you get over it."

Levi turned to his brother, a sharp retort stuck on his lips. Each hour brought her closer to going back home. He knew it, but until now, it hadn't made him so antsy. His chest tingled with the memory of her body lying against him last night. One look at the couch and he remembered holding her in the dark, soothing her tremors by stroking her hair.

What if the dark never goes away?

Damn him for being too drunk to try to get a little more information out of her last night. Aware that his brother was staring, Levi threw off the shower idea and headed to the kitchen for coffee.

"I won't need to get over it." He pulled a mug off the rack, set it down, and reached for the carafe. He lifted it, but didn't pour, the thought of coffee suddenly leaving a bitter taste in his mouth. He did need to get over something: everything that stood between Carrie and him. She'd slept on his chest and allowed him to soothe her fears, given him the taste of her lips without hesitation. They couldn't have that level of intimacy without some resolution. He'd hold on to those sweet pieces, but he didn't want to see her drive away without having wiped the slate clean.

"I gotta go." He came around the breakfast counter, looking for his keys.

Cole grabbed Levi's arm and rolled his eyes. "I figured. For Christ's sake, take a shower first. You smell like a bar."

After taking his brother's advice, Levi hurried outside only to find his truck gone. With a curse, he grabbed his cell and called Tucker, the first likely suspect.

"Where the hell is my truck?"

"Good morning to you, too, pretty boy." Tucker swallowed, strong coffee probably. "My ass is nice and toasty. Love these seat warmers."

Levi clenched his eyes. "*Why* do you have my truck?"

"Mine's stuck in the mud in the west pasture. Dug 'er down pretty deep."

"And you're taking my truck to…?"

"The west pasture."

Levi hung up with a growl and went back inside, grabbed a set of keys he hadn't touched in a long time, and, on second thought, a couple of blankets. It was a shame, really, that he had to do this. All the rain and mud wasn't good for a beauty like her, yet as he went into the shed and saw Daisy waiting for him, his pulse picked up. His 1964 Chevy Apache was looking prettier than ever thanks to Tucker's hard work in getting her restored while Levi had been away. It had been a long time since he'd driven her—not since before he'd left for the marines. As he slid inside and started her up, he figured it was a little sentimental that he was driving Daisy over to see Carrie. They'd spent hours together in this truck.

No more kissing. Just friends.

Wicked rules, but he had to abide by them. Even if the feel of her against him, the soft vulnerability of her form pressed against his, was a sweetness he craved. Having a woman in his arms hadn't meant anything to him aside from a few short hours of pleasure. But not Carrie. She'd always been more.

Levi tapped the key fob hanging down from the ignition, watching it swing before backing out of the shed. Rolling down the window, he stuck his elbow out and tried to relax. The air was balmy, cathartic. By the time he pulled into Agate Falls, his spirits were high—short-lived when he spotted Carrie on the porch, her eyes narrowed at him as he parked.

As he opened the truck door and slipped out, she resumed whatever she'd been doing. He tried not to take it personally, but dang if it didn't seem like she was dismissing him. Walking up beside her, he spied three nails clenched between her lips, a hammer and a bench with a broken leg lying at her feet.

He shoved his hands in his pockets. "Can I help?"

Her hair fell over one shoulder in a white-blond mess, shielding her face, but leaving the slim length of her arm visible. Pale skin, the smooth line of muscle gliding as she picked up the hammer.

After ignoring him a moment longer, she finally gave him her attention. "No." She eyed Daisy and her expression softened.

The last time he'd felt this awkward around Carrie, he'd been fifteen and was gearing up to kiss her for the first time. "Take a ride with me."

"Can't. I've got things to do. So do you, boss." She turned her back, leaving no doubt it was intentional this time. Well, too bad, because he wasn't giving up. He was here to bare his soul, and she was going to damn well listen. Even if he had to follow her pigheaded butt around the ranch, talking to her back. At least it would be a nice view.

"I've got things to say, Carrie Lynn." That caught her attention, even as it made his throat go tight. She turned slowly to catch his eyes and hold tight. Yeah, he'd never been a talker, but he figured willingness to flap his jaw now might help his cause. Her lips parted just enough to pull him into the memory of her taste.

She reached for a box of nails and a pair of gloves. "Then say them."

Hardball? Fine. He shifted his weight from one foot to the other and spread his arms wide. "Fine. I'm sorry, Carrie Lynn. For everything I did that hurt you." If he had to reel her in with a preemptive apology, so be it. He was going to say it eventually…and surprisingly it hadn't hurt as much as he'd thought it would.

Her shoulders squared up. Each second that she didn't look at him or speak dragged on. He could stand and wait her out for hours. Emotional depth had never been his thing. He'd try now, though. He owed her, and himself, the chance at some kind of closure to their past.

Wordlessly, she dropped the hammer and walked to door. It squeaked loudly as she opened it and went in. He thought she was going to shut it in his face, but she peeked out. "Give me a minute."

He left the porch and leaned against Daisy, ankles and arms crossed, looking up at the clear, sunny sky. Finally, she came toward him with a sweater on and her hair pulled back.

"I thought you might bolt out the back door and ditch me," he teased, hoping to lighten things between them. Carrie gave a one-sided grin and went around to the passenger door and slid inside. "That was the plan." Figures.

Levi drove them away from the ranch, down a series of back roads until pavement turned to dirt. He made a series of turns that led them away from the flat ground and over hills and rough terrain.

"It's been a long time since I've been out here." The excitement in her voice eased him.

This was one of his favorite places—one he'd thought he could put behind him when he'd left for the military, but he'd been wrong. He hadn't forgotten anything that he'd loved.

Levi parked where the foot of the mountain rose above

them, a narrow stream crawling down the crags and rocks to the smooth expanse of grassland where it snaked into the distance. A faint rush of water floated on the warm air, but only someone who knew where to look would actually find its source. Carrie jumped out of the truck, her eager smile contagious.

"Come on," she said, tugging on his sleeve. He followed, the sound of rushing water getting louder as they approached the stream. A line of rocks made a modest footpath along the water's edge. They followed, keeping mostly out of the water, until they reached the base of the mountain. A six-foot wide crevice in the rock hugged them as they slipped inside it, daylight fading to nothing. Carrie faltered, her left foot slipping into the water. She reached behind her to grab hold of him. Levi balanced her with one hand while he pulled a small flashlight out of his shirt pocket with the other.

He clicked it on, washing the cavern in light. "Let me go first, Carrie. Then you can hang on to me while I shine the light." Stepping into the water, he bit back a gasp at the coolness of it, and picked his way in front of her. His shirt was pulled tight—she must have grabbed him with both hands— as he angled the beam ahead of him.

"It's okay, Sunshine. You want to keep going?"

"Of course. I just can't see very well."

Grabbing her hand, he squeezed. "I'm with you."

She moved closer, the warmth of her body pressing against his back. "Let's go."

The heavy fall of water became louder, but not overwhelmingly so. Above them, the cavern rose like a cathedral ceiling, a split in the top allowing the narrow, gentle waterfall to come down from the mountain above. The falls changed from year to year, depending on how frost caused the rocks above to shift. Now it was narrow and appeared easy to maneuver around, though some years, the only way to get behind the waterfall was to go straight through it.

Levi clicked off the light as daylight flooded the space. "Ready?" he asked.

"Ready."

They skirted the waterfall and got spattered with cool spray. Behind it, they stepped into a circular room veiled by the falls on one side. The Devil's Kettle. Brilliant light shone down from an open ceiling as a blast of warm, humid air swirled around them. A basin lay in the center of the room, filled with water that came up from a hot spring in the ground. Usually deep enough to be chest-high, the Kettle was warm as bathwater, year round. Nature's private hot tub.

Bending to the water, Carrie dipped her hand inside.

"Perfect!" She stood, her shirt pressed against the delicate line of her ribs and waist. He wiped water droplets from his eyes, wanting a better view of how luscious she looked just then. He froze. Carrie unbuttoned her shirt, staring at him as the fabric fell open. Then she peeled it off.

The rush in his head wasn't from the water. Holding him with an unwavering look, she unbuttoned her jeans next and let them drop. Kicked them away on the ledge. Bare, except for the thin line of panties across her hip and the maybe-pink bra cupping her breasts, her body was willowy and graceful. She'd filled out, her hips flaring beautifully, her thighs lush and curved enough to make his mouth water.

Christ.

"I'm going for it, Levi!" He caught a flash of her hair billowing free from the ponytail before she slid chest-deep into the Kettle. His breath came out in a rush, his hands aching to touch her. He'd asked her to come with him so he could settle things between them before she went back to Wyoming. She was grinning at him, wearing nothing but her underwear. Hell, they could talk later.

Levi pulled his T-shirt off.

He was going for it, too.

Chapter Fifteen

She'd woken up in his arms, snuggled against him on the couch this morning. After long moments relishing the contentment his embrace provided, she'd carefully gotten up and left. It was cowardly, the way she'd slipped out, but necessary. She was falling hard, walking a line between allowing it and resisting it more. It was brutal, not knowing what to do, yet here she was, encouraging something to happen between them.

The thought of going back to Wyoming was depressing. The more she relived and experienced here, the worse her longing to stay became. She couldn't...the fear was still there telling her that it wasn't possible, that she needed the city in order to best take care of herself. She had a lot of fear where Levi was concerned, too, but it wasn't the same.

As each day passed, the apprehension she had over him faded a little. His smile and laugh reminded her why she'd loved him before. Then he'd do something unexpected, like comfort her fear of the dark, and she realized why she was starting to love him again.

She ducked her head beneath the tepid water, relishing

the lukewarm sensation on her scalp and skin before she surfaced. Levi's fingers were on the button of his jeans. She waited with anticipation to see if he'd finally take them off and let her see, but his hands fell away. Crouching, he slid into the water and disappeared beneath.

He surfaced, smoothing hair back from his eyes, the strong lines of his shoulders and chest glistening. Rooted in place by his beauty, she shivered hard as he came closer.

"Been waiting a long time for this," he said, taking her upper arms in his hands. A droplet of water trailed down his temple. She reached up and traced it with a finger, catching the drop on the curve of his cheek. His hand ran up and over her shoulder, to her neck, fingers warm as he gently ran them behind her ear and cradled her head in his palm.

"I used to dream about me and you being here." He licked his lower lip and looped a length of her hair around his finger. "I used to dream about you all the time. Every day, Carrie Lynn."

She mourned the chances they never had. All that time, she could have been there for him, not just as a memory but as the woman waiting for him to come home. The news about the war, pictures of men in uniform, and stories of wives left behind had been daily reminders of what she'd lost. If he'd asked her to be, she would have been the wife waiting, praying, for him to come home.

He took her face between his hands, the blue of his eyes startling from the frame of black lashes and filtered sunlight.

"And now?" She said, afraid to ask, afraid to push… afraid of the position the truth might put her in.

"I want you as much as I ever did. No…I want you *more*." His mouth was on hers before she could utter a word. Hard and soft. Demanding and giving—pulling her heart and fogging her brain. Carrie gripped his shoulders at the same time Levi hitched her up so her legs wrapped around his middle.

He braced her with arms under her butt while he devoured her mouth. A starving man—wanting this as much as she did. *Needing* it. She needed it. Levi was the piece that clicked inside her, the balm that could take the hurt and fear away.

He pulled back from her lips and placed soft, warm kisses over her jaw. "I planned on letting you go again. But damn it, Carrie, I don't want to."

Her thighs clenched around him. "Don't let me go." She pulled him back in for another kiss, tilting her head to align their lips as her embrace tightened around him. Pressed against his warm, wet skin and rocked by the soft current, she felt reality narrow down to the feel of his body and the pleasure of his mouth.

Letting go now would crush her. All the pieces of her that had broken when he'd left and slowly knitted together with fragile lines would shatter, irreparably. Carrie pulled back, panting, her lips crying for more, but the truth making a louder demand. If they were going down this path, he needed to know what he was getting into.

"We need to have that talk."

His thumbs swept over her cheeks. "Anything you want to talk about, baby."

Gripping his wrists, she blinked away moisture from her lashes and the burn in her eyes.

"I'm going blind."

. . .

Every part of him went cold. Carrie blinked, waiting for some response, but he couldn't seem to make his lips work. Maybe the rush of water from the falls had blurred her words and he hadn't heard her correctly. With a trembling hand, she wiped at her eyes.

She hurried, looking down as if she were ashamed.

Cupping her chin, he brought her gaze back to him. "It's just a matter of time now before I lose all sight in the right, but the left… I should have time yet."

She started to tremble, either from her admission or the water cooling on her skin. "Carrie," he said gently. He'd meant to say more, but it wouldn't come. How could this be happening to her? All her years of dealing with her health, and now her vision, too? A tear rolled down her face, prompting his eyes to burn with emotion. Clasping her to his chest, Levi held her tightly, focusing on his breathing, on hers, until he felt calmer.

"Let's get out. I have blankets in the truck. I'll build a fire and we can talk." *Please don't tell me to take you home*, he thought, wanting more than anything to give her a chance to talk, to tell him, and to absorb what she said.

At her short nod, Levi guided her to the ledge and helped her jump up. He followed, using his arms to hike his butt up onto the ledge so he could swing his legs around—harder to do for him in soaked jeans than her in nothing but panties. As he spied her dressing out of the corner of his eye, it all became apparent. All the times she rubbed her right eye, as if it was irritated. How she often blinked and squinted on that side as if the light was too bright.

Signs that she'd been carrying around this heavy secret. He knew what it was like, not wanting anyone to know about your disability, because it was too painful to wonder how people would react, or judge. He was still wearing his jeans, wasn't he? Soaked and heavy because he'd been too nervous to take them off and let Carrie see the damage underneath.

When they were dressed, Levi clasped Carrie's hand and led her along the rocky path and back under the waterfall. Outside, daylight hung on by threads of red and orange.

At the truck, he put a hand to her back, willing her to look at him. Did she really worry that her condition would change his feelings? He was a poster boy for being broken. Noticing how she'd soaked through her jeans and T-shirt, his own wet clothes clinging coolly to his skin, he grabbed a blanket and the fire kit he'd always kept in Daisy, like a good Boy Scout.

"Come here, Sunshine." He unfolded the blanket and stepped to her side, glad when a grateful smile crossed her lips as he covered her shoulders with it. A few minutes later, he'd scooped out a small fire pit from the soil and lit tinder with flint and steel. Carrie stood quietly next to him as the kindling burst into flame. He fed it dry sticks, and just as daylight began to shift, the fire pit flickered with hungry, warm flames.

"Impressive." Carrie folded the blanket under her on the grass and sat. Holding up a finger to indicate a minute, Levi went back to the truck and pulled out his dry jeans, and changed into them with the bed of the truck between him and her. Grabbing another blanket, he joined her at the fire and threw on larger pieces of wood.

He sat so their knees touched. Warmth from the flames seeped straight through the denim and into his legs. "Does your dad know?"

She was watching the flames. "Not yet. I...I'm not ready to face his disappointment."

"How could he ever be disappointed by something like this? That's not him, Carrie."

When she hesitated, Levi took her hand in his and loosely threaded their fingers. He wished she weren't hurting, but he got it. The way her shoulders slumped a little and she seemed to be thinking of exactly what to say next, he had the hunch she hadn't discussed this with anyone lately, if ever.

Around them, the hushed call of birds and insects overlaid the soft trickle of the creek in the distance. Carrie rubbed her thumb along his. "You know he's always done everything possible to take care of me. He was so careful that I followed a good diet, and kept up with checking my blood sugar and taking my insulin just right. Whenever I got sick, he basically shut everything down to take care of me."

"I know."

Levi shifted on the blanket, remembering how easily Carrie's blood sugar used to get out of control. One little illness, a change in her diet, or too much physical activity could make it plummet.

"He thought getting me off the ranch would help, you know, so I wouldn't feel compelled to do more than I should. Suggesting that I go live with Aunt Mary and Barb was his way of making sure I was always looked after."

Pressure built up in Levi's chest. He knew that well, too. Darren had made him promise not to interfere with Carrie's going to live with her aunts, so she could attend college. He'd made him swear on his honor as a man, a Haywood, and a future marine that he'd let Carrie go. He looked away from her, watched the mesmerizing emptiness of the flames as they danced.

"But then I fell. Hit my head on the sidewalk and detached my right retina. The doctors tried to fix it, but the blood vessels in my eye were already damaged from the diabetes and it never healed properly."

Her lower lip tucked beneath her top teeth as she squeezed his fingers. "They're giving me another six months before I won't be able to drive anymore. I'm going to be impaired enough that it will completely change my life, Levi."

It made sense now why she'd been asking him about his own recovery. She'd always had an independent streak, with enough willfulness to make the devil pull his hair out. She was adaptable, strong. The naked fear in her tone suggested that none of those traits were holding her up through this. Being lost, not knowing how to navigate the changes or the mental games they played, caused a consuming kind of fear.

He knew well.

"If you haven't told your dad, who is helping you through

this?" He flipped her hand palm-up and placed a kiss in the center.

"He and my aunts know I hit my head, but I didn't tell them about my vision. I've been in denial about it until recently."

"Denial is vicious and it will tear you down. Let me help you, Sunshine." He kissed her wrist, pausing to feel the slight pound of her pulse beneath the tender skin. No matter what, she was vital, alive, her soul as beautiful as ever. The physical didn't matter as long as she kept her spirit.

"I have to go back, Levi," she whispered. A sob bubbled from her throat. "Don't you see? Once I can't drive, I lose my independence. Out here, there's nothing. No bus, no subway. No work, nothing. I'll be trapped. At least in the city, I can get around. I can... I can still *live*."

With a gentle yank, he pulled her into his arms. She shifted her hips to accommodate the movement, nearly settling onto his lap. Each second, each word from her mouth punctuated his desire, his need to have her stay. He despised desperation, especially when he had no concrete solution to offer her. He could provide for her, sure, but beyond that, how could he make sure the ranch didn't become her prison?

"Don't talk about leaving. Not when I just got you back." He tipped her head, the silky, damp mass of her hair cascading over his hands.

"I hated how you left me," she blurted. "I would have waited for you, gone with you anywhere."

Levi wanted to turn in on himself and shield her from the pain he'd caused. But he'd resolved to man-up a long, long time ago, and he was going to own the past for what it was— the past—and do what he needed to for what lay ahead.

"I'm sorry." He cupped her face "I. Am. Sorry."

Everything he'd buried ripped to the surface, emotions so strong they clogged his throat and beat his heart with raging fists. Torn between old anger and the desperate need for her acceptance, Levi rained kisses over her cheeks, the bridge of her nose, lingered over the corner of her mouth.

Carrie gripped his wrists, her voice a broken sob. "I missed you."

Levi swallowed hard, kissed her harder. "God, Carrie, I missed you, too."

"Why didn't you tell me sooner you were leaving?"

Levi slid his hands down her sides and gripped her hips. He leaned his forehead against hers. "Because if you'd begged me to take you with me, I would have. And I couldn't do that. I promised your father."

"What?"

He wiped her tears with the slide of a thumb, feeling like she was crying for the both of them. "I couldn't take you away from the safety of your family. I knew Darren hoped you'd go to Wyoming. I'd be gone for months while you waited at the military base, away from everyone. I couldn't do it, Carrie."

Twenty was young enough to still be selfish, but old enough to be understand that he needed to look out for her and not just himself.

"As much as I loved you, wanted you, I couldn't wrap my head around any reason being good enough for that, Carrie. I would have worried about you every second, and what…what kind of life would that have been for two kids like us?"

Maybe Darren had recognized the restlessness, the yawning ache inside Levi that needed to be quenched. Going into the marines was his one chance to experience life away from the ranch—to spread his wings and figure out what he really wanted from life. Despite all the pain it had caused Carrie and him, he wouldn't change it. Leaving Paint River had turned a restless kid into a man who knew the importance of the land, of growing roots.

He knew now that he wanted his feet on Montana soil until the day they dug a hole and put him in it.

"Don't be mad at your father. He's a smart man, though I didn't like him much when he strong-armed me into giving you up. At that time, it was the right thing to do."

She pulled back, her brow furrowed into soft lines. "What pisses me off is that the two of you took it upon yourselves to keep *me* out of the discussion. Do you know how many times I've had decisions made for me, as if diabetes has somehow made me mentally incapable?" Carrie moved to get up, but Levi wrapped his arms around her.

Her eyes flashed. "The ranch, for instance. I come home to find out you basically own it."

"I did it for you. Jesus, Carrie, do you think I'd let your childhood home go to auction? The minute I was able to get my feet on the floor and stand up without a fucking walker, I was determined to come to you. To find you, to *see you again*. Then I found out about the ranch, and I figured…maybe you'd see how sorry I am."

He brought her to his chest. Wetness pooled where his fingers cupped her jaw. Trembling, she sank into his body. Emotions pumped through him, bouncing and colliding with each other. The closer he got to her, the more everything faded down to the simple realization that he'd stepped right back in love with her. With greedy hands, he pulled Carrie fully into his lap. Her legs went around his hips.

She was warm and vibrant in his arms. Little kisses trailed over her hair until they met the skin of her temple. His fingers skimmed behind her left ear until they disappeared into her hair, his lips dotting her forehead with adoring kisses.

"I never stopped caring about you, Sunshine. I learned to push it away, but it was always there, with each breath."

Her hands smoothed over his chest until she met the hem of his shirt and lightly tugged it up. He hissed a breath as she touched his ribs beneath the fabric and leaned close to his ear.

"Show me."

Chapter Sixteen

She hoped Levi would throw her onto her back and rip her shirt open. That's what the pure lust running through her craved. Instead, he placed a soft kiss on her lips before he drew back.

Taking his hand, Carrie took a short breath to slow her racing nerves before placing his palm on her breast. Seemed a lifetime ago, or maybe someone else's lifetime, that they'd been seventeen and Levi had laid her down inside the barn, tucked into a corner of the hayloft, on thick blankets like the ones he'd brought tonight.

She'd fumbled; he'd soothed. Those hours they'd spent in each other's arms that first time, and all the times after, were safe, comfortable, perfect; exquisite—and nothing she'd experienced since had matched.

Levi straightened, with one hand on her lower back. He pushed her forward, his lips finding her neck to trail firm kisses over her skin as her hips slid forward until they were locked together. Hips to hips, chest to chest. The fire crackled, sending up a flare of sparkling embers as their lips met. The first kiss was gentle but quickly changed as Levi cradled the back of her head, tipping her to the side so his mouth could devour hers completely.

He meshed their lips with long, hard, nearly bruising pressure that balanced between raw and controlled. Meeting her tongue with his, he explored her mouth as he softened the kiss, giving her a blip of needy panic that he would restrain himself. She didn't want restraint. She wanted his raw passion—all that heat and strength and pure power that had always emanated from him, but he'd rarely displayed with her.

Maybe he didn't feel as powerful anymore—maybe she needed to remind him he was still strong; perfect and everything she'd always desired.

"I'm not fragile," she rushed. His kiss turned fierce, his fingers tugging at the buttons of her shirt. When that proved too slow, he nudged her arms up and pulled it over her head. Still damp from the waterfall, her bra clung to her breasts. The warmth of his hands soaked through the wet fabric, making her shudder.

Carrie leaned into his touch, closed her eyes to better absorb each sensation as Levi lowered one bra strap, his fingers drawing lazily down her shoulder. Turning to the other side, he did the same, leaving perfect rows of heat where each finger imprinted into her skin.

Levi pulled her into another kiss as his hands looped around her to unfasten the bra. His lips marked a path down the side of her throat while his touch hovered over her breasts—stealing her breath in anticipation and longing. Just when she was about to vocalize her need, he slid a hand to her hip and leaned her back, cupping her left breast, his mouth closing over the rigid peak.

Carrie arched, forcing her hips forward so her pelvis leaned into his hard length. The simultaneous sensation of his hard erection and soft mouth nearly paralyzed her with need. It had been eons since she'd been touched, or even wanted to be. That it was happening now with the man who'd repeatedly haunted her fantasies was almost too much for her brain to process. Her insides quivered with anticipation, like being afraid of heights but standing close to the ledge… waiting for the moment your eyes close and you lean forward and simply fly.

She pulled up the hem of his shirt, urging him back enough to yank it up and over his head. The warmth of Levi's chest saturated every inch of her torso against his as he brought her to him. He devoured her mouth, his hands gliding up and down her back. And then he was urging her up, letting their kiss meet and linger as long as possible before she stood.

He found the button on her shorts, hooking his thumbs in the waistband, panties included, and yanked them down. "Girl, the only thing I want to see on you is tan lines." The cool air that washed over her belly and thighs had a short life span as Levi grabbed her hips and pulled her back over his lap. She straddled him, began to lower onto his lap, but a squeeze of his hands stopped her. Looking down, she noticed his gaze was slowly roaming her middle…the very center of her almost in perfect alignment with his mouth.

Anticipation and liquid heat rippled through her limbs. And then his hands smoothed over the rise of her buttocks, nails lightly raking over the backs of her thighs. Cupping her backside, he pulled her closer. Her hands found his shoulders because she needed something, anything, to support herself. As if knowing, Levi wrapped an arm beneath her bottom as his lips touched her lower belly.

Soft. One simple touch of his lips. Electricity exploded beneath that gentle touch. Quivering, desperate for more, Carrie clenched her fingers into the soft-hard flesh of his shoulders and tipped her hips so slightly, offering. Surrendering.

He caressed her hips, his fingers lightly teasing along the sensitive rise of her hip bone, to her belly button…a vertical line down…

"I don't see any tan lines, Sunshine." A hot stream of breath punctuated where his finger stopped just above her curls. "Maybe I need to look closer."

She couldn't drum up a vocal response, only a physical one—leaning into the press of his mouth when he placed a kiss. Shaking, Carrie held her breath as he brushed her curls with his fingers, his mouth touching those insane little kisses over every inch of her belly.

Panting, positive she'd never be able to stand without assistance again, Carrie fumbled with the zipper on his jeans as he rose back over her. He groaned when the fly finally fell open and she parted it wider before trying to pull the waist down. He gripped her wrist with a small shake of his head.

"Keep them on."

Beside them, the fire crackled—a perfect echo to the desire racing through her. She wanted to see him, all of him. Nothing between them but the night air. Yet, not wanting anything to dampen the moment, she smiled and ran her hand down the length of his cock beneath his boxers. They had time to get comfortable enough to expose everything— he would, she had no doubt. And she'd accept him no matter what he had hiding under the denim, because she absolutely couldn't fathom doing anything else.

In a swift move, she'd pulled down his boxers, freeing him completely. They both made little noises at the same time as she gripped him hard, remembering and experiencing. Before she could stroke him, Levi positioned her above him, brought her down with a softly questioning look in his eyes.

"Oh yes, baby," she reassured him, letting him lower her,

widening her legs to steady herself as he entered—slowly, but with a firm glide. As her body adjusted to him, her brain remembered how it felt to have Levi inside her. Only, this was different—fuller, more meaningful. When she had him completely, Carrie let the fog in her brain take over as pleasure tingled through every nerve path in her body, lighting her up in a way she'd never been before, making her nearly crazed in her need to have him.

She clung to him, arms around his neck, nipples brushing against the warmth of his chest as he moved, reaching a place inside her that set off a barrage of sparks each time he touched. He wasn't stroking her clit, but it felt like he was, each upward motion pushing her closer to an orgasm. It was an illusion, a figment of her mind, something, because *this* had never happened like this before.

"Oh, God, Levi." She moaned into his neck, fingers digging into his back. His breathing was erratic and hard, the muscles along his collarbone straining as he guided her up and down with fierce, fluid motion.

"Come on, girl, give it to me." And then his fingers were between her legs, gently rubbing the spot that jumped to life at his touch. The simultaneous stimulation was almost too much—almost—as her body wanted to give up and just *feel* but wouldn't allow her to stop moving. Grabbing his wrist, Carrie wanted to push his hand away, yet hold him there… edging the rim of that explosive pleasure she knew was there. If she could just fall…

"Please, Carrie Lynn." The heady, broken plea pushed her that much closer, until she circled it, danced around it. He gently bit her shoulder, his fingers making one long, firm stroke and she went for it. Let go. Shattered in his arms.

His name flew from her lips as she crushed her chest to his, rocking her hips against his touch as his own release followed. Like he'd been waiting for her. Lost in sensation,

Carrie had no idea how long they stayed like that, entwined together, breathing hard. When her skin began to cool, she looked up from his shoulder, and his arms loosened from around her.

His heavily lidded eyes crinkled at the corners. Pulling her in by the chin, Levi kissed her softly, their bodies still locked in a lazy way that made it clear neither of them was in a hurry to let the connection end. He brushed hair away from her cheeks with a reverent look, one arm cradling her hips with a strength that let her know she was secure. The way he was searching her face, though, made her think he was looking for reassurance.

How could you convey to someone that you'd never felt so gloriously alive in your entire life? That every touch, every moment, every breath had been absolute perfection? Carrie tilted her head and deepened the kiss, hoping she could display all the feelings in a way words never could. With a shuddering breath, Levi wrapped her in his arms and they clung together, the crackling fire making Carrie fuzzily aware that night had completely fallen. She smiled and let out a cleansing breath, melting into Levi's support, her body making a sweet descent from high passion to pleasurable closeness. Let night come.

For the first time in a long while, she wasn't afraid of the dark.

Chapter Seventeen

"Where the hell were you last night?"

Levi came down the porch steps and stopped short. His jaw tightened at the sight of his truck covered in mud, huge dried chunks clinging to the sides and caking the wheel wells. It had been well after midnight by the time he'd gotten Carrie home, sat around in a lazy glow with her tucked under his arm on the couch, and made it back to Paint River. He'd been too jacked in a post-sex high to notice his truck then.

Tucker met him on the bottom step, palms out. "I'm going to wash her right now, so settle down." His brother's eyes narrowed, a suggestive grin on his lips. "So, about last night…"

Levi punched his brother on the shoulder as he passed, but he couldn't keep a grin off his own lips. Yeah, about last night. He wasn't yet convinced it had really happened. If not for the excellent replay of Carrie's legs around him, her body moving with his, the sounds she made, he might have believed it had been just another dream. But no dream had ever been that tangible, that exquisite.

"Why are you so worried about it?"

"Because you missed the family dinner. Too busy to check your cell phone, huh?"

Levi groaned. He'd completely forgotten his family was gathering in Missoula to celebrate his mother's upcoming wedding. He was walking her down the aisle, for crying out loud. He should have remembered. God, she was going to kill him.

"She's going to kill you."

"Yeah."

"Cole must have called you twenty times."

"Hmmmm, yeah." Levi pulled his neglected phone from his back pocket and turned it on. The notification light began to flash like it was having a seizure. Twenty-three messages, actually.

"I said you were getting laid and to leave you be."

He put the phone back in his pocket. "Classy, Tuck. Classy."

Tucker shrugged one shoulder. "I've got your back, bro." With that, his brother went to the mud-encrusted truck and grabbed something from the front seat. He came back and thrust papers at Levi. "The contractor stopped late afternoon. Dropped these off for you."

The prints showed a mock-up of the camping space slated for the adjoining land between Paint River and Agate Falls. Flipping through each paper, Levi could easily envision the beautiful layout on the prints coming to life. Tastefully designed, the mixture of modern amenities like a luxurious bathhouse and a mini waterpark and playground combination for families, with the rugged backdrop of mountain range, trees, and creek, would create massive appeal.

Perfect. It's exactly what they'd wanted to put in at Paint River, but currently lacked the space for. Now, he just had to convince Darren it was a good use of his land. The profit worksheet alone should provide enough push. Agate Falls needed a sustainable future, and this was one big way to get it.

"Thanks, Tucker."

His brother nodded and took the porch stairs two at a time. Levi took a big breath of damp morning air, taking in the haze of mist floating over the peaks in the distance. The air had a purplish hue, brought to life by rays of the sun trying to burn through the fog. This view, this incredible nature, was what tourists loved. What they loved more was being pampered while they enjoyed the outdoors. Around him, the ranch was already awake and moving. The guest cabins had started to fill up and guest vehicles came and went. By summer, this place would be a mass of tourists, people constantly filtering in and out to go horseback riding, or have a cattle drive experience, or take a guided hike or fishing trip. They offered it all here.

But where was the limit? One more little tip in the wrong direction and they might as well fold up ranching save for a token to entertain the out-of-towners. He rolled the papers. Did he really want to subject Agate Falls' good ranching land to the same?

He thought of the Waites' old barn, the first structure put up on what would become a ten-thousand-acre ranch. Weathered, worn, it had refused to succumb to time and elements, standing crooked, but firm. Just like Agate Falls was now…injured, but still standing.

Another thought crossed his mind. Maybe there was a way he could bring in the secondary income the ranch needed without taking away from the land.

"Better come in and say morning to Ma before she decides not to let you walk her down the aisle after all." Tucker clomped down the stairs, a coffee mug in one hand and three doughnuts in the other.

Levi blankly watched Tucker get in his truck and pull away. His mind flooded with a possibility he hadn't considered before. Excitement coursed through him as the plan started to come together. He needed to tell Carrie…but not yet. Not until he had more information. No, he was better off keeping this to himself a while.

What he couldn't keep quiet was the pulsing fact that he didn't want her to leave.

The wedding was in a week, and she was leaving shortly. Even if they hadn't made love yesterday, he'd still be at war over letting her go. They'd made no promises, no proclamations of love, though he'd felt it in every touch of her hand, every breath against his skin. He'd survived a blast that had nearly taken his legs, learned to walk again, and quieted the nightmares in his mind. He'd been torn up, on the brink of a complete mental breakdown, and had been pulled back into life by the love and strength of his family.

His entire family would wrap around Carrie, too, he knew they would. He'd be there to hold her up, to push her through and to keep the light in her life. He needed to convince her to stay.

Going back inside, he dug out the papers he was looking for, filtering through them and really reading them for the first time.

"Holy shit," he uttered before he picked up the phone. This just might work.

· · ·

A bang sounded from outside, followed by distant male voices. Her blood warmed as she recognized Levi's tone. Holding back a sneeze from the dust, she ducked her head against the low attic ceiling and went to the dormer window. He was talking with two ranch hands, and slapped one on the shoulder and laughed at something he'd said. It wasn't lost on her that he'd taken on this role for her—to help her and Darren out as much as himself. He was suited to being in charge, to getting things done. And he seemed to love it. Levi fit here.

Just as he'd always fit her. After all this time, he could be the perfect puzzle piece, falling right into place as if he'd never been misplaced. Her body was alive with the memory of his touch, his kiss. He'd held her long into the night after they'd gotten back to Agate Falls, talking, sharing stories and bits and pieces of his life away from her. She'd done the same, realizing things she'd thought were insignificant or boring were fresh and new to him.

Well into the early-morning hours, they'd been trying to share six years of their lives as quickly as possible. Probably because time was dwindling down until she left and all this would go back to a hazy dream. So she'd stopped talking and simply enjoyed the feel of him wrapped around her until he carefully untangled them a few hours before dawn.

There were no regrets over what they'd shared yesterday. It would hurt later, when she was gone, but she'd do it all again. With a heavy sigh, Carrie moved away from the window and back to the stack of boxes she was sorting. She'd made the decision to be intimate with Levi, and nothing that perfect had room for overthinking and worry to tear it down.

Rummaging through the boxes, she pulled out little mementos she wanted to take with her, and made a small pile. Satisfied, she put everything else back and turned her attention to the large stained glass panel she'd uncovered a few days ago.

The usually vibrant hues of the sunflowers and cardinals were dull, covered by a fine misting of dust. She'd worked countless hours to make it. The process had been cathartic in the heartbreaking time after Levi had left her. Carrie used the edge of her shirt and wiped dust away from one of the cardinals. Instantly, the red went from drab to ruby.

She'd created something beautiful when she'd been broken, and it had survived intact all this time. Dings marred the wooden frame. Small nicks in the glass and chips in the lead beading displayed that the panel had seen rough times, but the imperfections didn't make it less. With a little care, it would shine like it had before.

Carrie leaned back and traced a finger along the top of the frame. Like the stained glass, maybe she and Levi just needed a bit of tending to make them strong again. Hope flooded through her at the thought. She was being given a second chance with a man who could help her deal with the changes her medical condition could bring.

Inspired to polish up the panel, she stood and lugged it to the door and out onto the landing. It wasn't heavy, just bulky, and with three flights of stairs to come down, she'd have to pick her way carefully.

"Carrie Lynn?" Levi's voice sounded from the bottom of the staircase, startling her. She maneuvered down the first set of stairs. Her pulse picked up, but it wasn't from carrying the stained glass.

"Yeah?"

"Come on down a minute?"

She cocked an eyebrow. "How about you come up here?"

There was a pause. "My boots are muddy."

Readjusting the panel, Carrie went down the second flight. "You traipse through the house with muddy boots, but you can't come up? Hope you're good with a...mop." She stopped on the landing, getting her first good look at him. A bouquet of purple and yellow flowers was clutched in his left hand.

Jet-black blades of hair spiked along his forehead and curled over his ears. His red-and-black flannel shirt was unbuttoned, showing off a painted-on gray T-shirt underneath, and the low rise of his jeans. This messy country thing he had going on was totally working for her. Swarthy lengths of skin showed along his forearms from his rolled-up sleeves, the corded muscle nicely defined.

His cocky smile got bigger. "You're staring, Sunshine."

"If you saw yourself from a female perspective, you'd be staring, too."

"That right?"

"Mmm-hmm." Setting the stained glass against the wall on the landing, she came down the last stairs. A muscle in his brow twitched, followed by an impatient shifting of his feet that made her wonder what exactly he had in mind when she reached the bottom. Three steps from him she paused and tilted her head to catch the brilliance of his eyes.

"You look like you're up to no good, Levi Haywood."

"That's what these flowers are for."

He came up two steps, boots perfectly clean, she noticed. He took her hand as he went back down to the floor, then gave her a gentle tug that propelled her into his arms. Carrie squealed, her breath catching in her throat.

"You're making me wait way too long for this kiss, woman." She was vaguely aware of the flowers falling to the floor as Levi hitched her up onto his waist, urging her legs around his hips. Her knee-length skirt bunched over the tops of her thighs. One arm supported her beneath her rear, the other wrapped around her head.

Her response was a nonsensical sound, because his lips were on hers with a bruising, luscious kiss. He walked her back the short distance to the wall and pressed her against it. Carrie tightened her thighs against the hard curve of his waist, positive she was going to fall. His tongue made a sensual sweep along hers, his lips urging her lips farther apart. His hand lightly followed the contour of her shoulder, down her arm to trace her ribs and the curve of her waist. She shifted, bringing her bottom in contact with the hard ridge in his jeans. Levi groaned and pulled at the hem of her shirt, lifting it and sliding his hand beneath.

Skin on skin—the rough pads of his fingers over the sensitive, tender flesh of her abdomen made a wandering path over her body until all the clothed parts were begging to be freed.

His hands cupped her breasts, and she was done. Lost. She put her arms in between his and nudged his hands away from her chest. Her breasts ached for contact as she grabbed Levi's flannel shirt and tried peeling it over his shoulders. With the force of his hips alone, he held her against the wall and shrugged out of the shirt. Taking her wrists, he stretched her arms up above her head.

Taking her shirt in both hands, he pulled it up with a slow, teasing pace that made her libido squirmy and demanding. As each inch of her skin was bared, her breasts ached more and that spot between her legs—the one he had his pelvis wedged against just right—was ready to go postal.

"Sucks to wait, doesn't it, Sunshine?" The shirt flipped up and made a path over her arms, covering her face. Anticipating he'd pull the fabric free and toss it aside, Carrie squirmed in protest a bit when he didn't. Soft, wet lips pressed against her collarbone. Nibbling along her clavicle, Levi bit just hard enough to send zings of pleasure-pain down her chest. With one forceful pull, the shirt cleared her body and his chest pressed into hers.

"Right here." He growled, nearly ripping the strap of her bra from her shoulders. It tugged against her flesh with a sharp pull, and then it fell, lowering the cup and baring her breast.

"Yes, here," she repeated, arching her back in search of his mouth on her pebbled nipple.

He pulled the other strap down. "Right now." Against the wall, at the base of the stairs in the hallway. She couldn't have cared less.

"Anywhere, Levi. Whenever you want." Her fingers found his hair and pulled his head down until his hot breath assaulted her breasts. One more desperate tug and his lips closed around her left nipple. Sensations became a flurry from his lips and his wandering, delicious touch, until Carrie thought the very center of her would explode. His skin smelled like fresh soap, with the faint flavor of hard work and sunshine when she cruised his neck with her lips.

Her body must have conveyed the edge she was on, because Levi worked the fastener of his jeans with one hand while supporting her with the other. Consumed with the dizziness of need, she tried to move back to allow him room. But Levi took over, holding her hip and moving the thin strip of her panties aside. His hips moved back as he repositioned just slightly—just enough to align them perfectly.

And when the tip of his cock pressed against her entrance, Carrie arched forward with the elation of anticipation. But Levi palmed her hip and stopped her motion, catching her eyes. His brows knit together, adding to the strain of withheld passion on his face.

"God, Levi." Determined, wanting, she traced his lower back with her hands, pushing the open waist of his jeans down farther, and raked her nails over the firm rise of his ass.

Carrie tipped her pelvis up and then moved her hips down, bringing the tip of him inside and making them both gasp. He was lost—he knew it; she could tell as he closed his eyes, the veins on the sides of his neck straining. He was long and full, and with each glide in, she didn't think she could take any more of him. But she did, welcoming each thrust until her body adjusted and he was moving along that sweet spot deep inside. It was all-consuming, the licks and bursts of pleasure he rent out of her, bringing her closer to release with each thrust.

He groaned, a deep, riveting sound in her ear. "You always did come so easily, Sunshine." Levi pounded into her, his hip bones biting into her thighs with the promise of bruises. Marks. He could mark her anywhere, however many times he wanted. She already belonged to him. Completely. Absolutely. "Give it to me, Carrie." His hand moved between them, his fingers finding her clit with a firm stroke.

She cried out as a sudden, ecstatic wave of pleasure rolled through her, not caring if the whole ranch heard what Levi was doing to her. Instead of leaving her fulfilled, the orgasm had her aching for more.

"Harder..." Nearly frantic, Carrie urged him to thrust harder, digging her fingers into his ass, begging with little pants. And he did, ramming her into the wall, gliding against that spot deep inside her until she didn't know what to do with her hands, or how to move to make the near-painful buildup stop. Until suddenly she found her tipping point and fell into another bursting spiral of release. Levi cursed, gripping her hips until his fingertips burned into her flesh as he pulsed inside her with his own completion.

It was a while before either of them moved. Levi sagged against her with his forearms braced on the wall. Slowly, she unwrapped her legs from around him and slid down until her feet were on the floor. She touched his cheek and smiled. He smiled back with the reassurance that this was enough. This quiet, comfortable bubble around them was enough.

She didn't watch as he fixed his jeans, afraid the denim had fallen enough to display his thighs. She didn't want to make him uncomfortable. When he was ready to show her, he would. And truthfully, she wasn't sure she was ready to see that part of him yet. Maybe it was selfish, but she wanted a little more time in the happy delirium before reality had to come back.

"You know," Levi said as he zipped his jeans. "I came in here for a reason."

She smoothed her skirt with a wink. "You mean that wasn't it?"

He took her hand and gently rubbed his thumb over the back. "This is more than physical for me, Carrie."

The sincerity in his voice made her throat go tight. She reached up on tiptoe and kissed him, just once, softly. "Well then, what did you have in mind?"

"You're going bull riding."

Chapter Eighteen

Levi pushed his plate away and crossed his arms over the red-and-white-checkered tablecloth. One half a barbecue chicken, a baked potato—make that two, because he'd eaten Carrie's, too—salad, and whatever else had been on his plate later, and he was done.

The Big Sky Roadhouse was known for its chicken, and man, had Levi missed it. The restaurant was double level, with a circular balcony above to show off the second dining area. Down here, there was sawdust on the floor, a huge bar with an even bigger jukebox, and in the corner, Willie, the mechanical bull.

It was old, the black leather covering torn with the metal body beneath showing through. There was only one reason patrons rode Willie, and that was to earn a big old slab of chocolate stout cake. Complete an eight-second ride and get a slice of heaven made from double dark chocolate with Guinness in both the batter and the frosting. Hell to the yes. He'd never be too full for that.

Leaning his chair back on two legs, he eyed Carrie's plate.

She'd hardly touched a thing. She put a hand to her stomach and frowned before taking a long drink of water.

"You okay?"

She waved a hand around her face. "Just heartburn." Draining her glass, Carrie refilled it from the carafe. "I have chicken here, you know." She pushed the plate toward him, but Levi stopped her with his hand. "Good Lord, no. Trying to kill me?"

Her eyelids went half closed in a sexy, amused kind of way that was more comical than seductive. He loved it. "No, just fueling you up for later."

He snagged her hands with one of his and leaned over his elbows on the table. "In that case, you'd better eat up, girlie, or you won't be able to keep up with me." They shared an intimate look that he enjoyed—really enjoyed—but served as a reminder that he'd meant what he'd said earlier. This thing between them wasn't just physical. Everything about her was important to him, and there was so much he didn't know.

Levi searched her face, enjoying the beautiful lines and dips. Her eyes flickered down, her cheeks going pink. "You're staring."

He laughed before bringing her knuckles to his lips. "If you saw yourself from a male perspective, you'd be staring, too." She opened her hands and entwined their fingers, the sensation of her palms fitting perfectly in his making him forget that they were in public. In that moment, they were alone and time was being kind…going slow so he could savor her.

Hell, hadn't be been savoring each moment with her as if it could be their last? She withdrew a hand to gingerly rub at her right eye, blinking fast as if she were trying to clear her vision. His heart lurched. Carrie was adept at hiding signs of her declining sight, except for small moments like this when an apparently normal action like rubbing her eye meant something besides simple irritation.

One day, she'd be blind. Maybe not completely, but enough that she needed someone with the stability, love, and heart to be her companion through it. Damn well no other man would have that role but him.

A waitress stopped at their table to clear their plates. When she was gone, he kept his voice low. "I don't want you to go back to Wyoming."

A blank look crossed her face before her forehead scrunched. "Levi... I—"

"Before you say anything, just answer me this. What are your biggest fears about staying?"

She shook her head, withdrawing her hand, leaving his fingers cool and his palm empty. "You can't fix it, Levi. You can't fix this."

"I know you're scared, Sunshine. I get it. If anyone understands your fear, it's me. Don't you...don't you think that maybe, we were brought back together for a reason? Maybe because with my legs, and...and your eyes, we understand each other. *Perfectly.*"

Her face softened. "I was thinking that same thing this morning." Another soft shake of her head and she dropped her eyes.

"You'll never be alone, Carrie. I'm here, your dad is here. My family loves you. And when the time comes, we'll work to keep as much of your independence as possible." He moved to stand beside her and dropped to one knee. Threading their fingers, he licked his lower lip and took a breath. "Whatever you need, whatever you want, *I'll be there* for you."

She closed her eyes as a wave of conflict crossed her features. He'd never been a begging man, had never had the inclination to plead for anything, not even his life, but he was at that point now. "Sophie is a highly trained paramedic and keeps meds and things at the house. She's usually around, but if she's not, the new first responder crew in Greenbrook carries diabetic medication."

Her hands squeezed his, and when she swallowed hard, Levi cupped her cheek. "And when, if, your sight gets to the point where you can't drive or manage the same way, we'll manage. Together. I let you go once. That was one time too many."

Carrie leaned into his touch, moisture gleaming in her eyes.

"Can I get you guys anything else?" A soft voice beside them made Levi aware of the unusual scene they were making. He stood, smiling at the waitress.

"It's Willie time."

The server gave an agreeing nod. "Great! I'll meet you over there."

Disappointed that their moment was broken, Levi held out a hand to Carrie. She wiped at her eyes before taking it and walked easily into his arms for an embrace. "It *was* one time too many," she whispered in his ear before pulling back and placing a sweet kiss on his lips. He was about to ask her if that meant she'd think about staying, but he hadn't played all his cards yet. He was saving the best for last.

"Come on. I'm ready for my stout cake, woman."

"No way." She rolled her eyes good-naturedly.

With a light pull, he led her to the roped-off square in the corner where Willie sat. He gave a sweep of his arm and nodded his head as if she should go get on.

Hands on her slim hips, she feigned indignation. "I have to do the work so you can have cake?"

Levi shrugged and nudged her closer to the bull. Whispering low in her ear, he relished the little shiver that went through her. "I gave you two orgasms earlier. You owe me."

Carrie whapped him on the chest with the back of her

hand. The waitress came over with the key for the bull.

"Get on up, sweetheart." The waitress indicated that Carrie should get on Willie, but she didn't. Instead, she grabbed the front of Levi's shirt and pulled him close. His pulse kicked up as his chest pressed into hers. With her left hand, she grabbed the small sign that contained the bull-riding rules and turned it away so he couldn't read it.

"No," he said. Riding a real horse was torture enough on his legs. He didn't need a go-round on a piece of leather with protruding metal bits.

"Yes."

"Sign says no doubling up."

The waitress cleared her throat and looked up at the ceiling, pulling the sign behind her body. "What sign?" Carrie high-fived the waitress before slipping onto the bull. Levi glanced around, realizing no one was paying them any attention. He ran a hand over Carrie's lower back, loving her body heat through the thin fabric, as he moved closer, swung his right leg over and hopped up. It was fluid, and easy and painless. Gripping Carrie's hips, he pulled her roughly back until she settled between his thighs. She moaned-sighed, a sound she made just for him, and he relished it.

"Hit it." The waitress turned the machine on. Levi let his body adjust to the sway and ran his arms under Carrie's to put one hand against her middle. Holding her firmly against him, he barely recognized that the bull's antics didn't increase. They stayed at a slow, laughable bounce and swerve, barely enough to require that they squeeze their legs to hang on.

He braced himself to Carrie anyway, inhaling the sweetness of her hair and the feel of her body against his chest. This was ridiculous—him and her on this stupid bull. For what? Cake.

He brushed her hair aside and placed a single, simple kiss on the base of her neck. It might be ridiculous, but it was *fun*.

She'd gotten him on this damn bull, and she was in his arms, anchoring him.

The bull swerved to the left, the trickiest motion it had made yet, making them bounce and grab for purchase. And then it slowed, swaying softly until it finally stopped. Carrie was wedged perfectly between his legs, her hand covering his against her belly as she turned to look over her shoulder at him. Levi leaned in until his lips found her ear, and gave it a gentle tug.

"You know what I'm most afraid of?" Her voice wavered, the tone low, intimate.

"What?"

"Not being able to see your beautiful face." Her arm looped behind his head, holding him to her. Levi clenched his eyes shut, absorbing the stab of bittersweet pleasure and pain that her words rent through his chest.

"You won't need to see me to know how much I love you." He held his breath as soon as the words were out, but there was no regret, no second-guessing. "I love you, Carrie Lynn."

Carrie's body stiffened and it gave him pause. Maybe he shouldn't have—

"I love you, too." She struggled to turn to fully face him. He slipped down instead, pulling her off the contraption and right into his arms, finding her lips as a cheer went up from the people around them. Damn. They'd had an audience after all.

Levi pulled back, never taking his eyes off her. "We'll take the cake to go."

• • •

"I'm not leaving tonight." Levi shrugged out of his jacket, then reached for hers. Carrie set the cake box down on the kitchen table, going still as he walked behind her and removed her coat. His fingers made a slow descent over her shoulders, bringing her skin to life.

"Good. I don't want you to go."

"Mmm-hmm," he replied in a gravelly tone. A tingly caress followed the length of her spine and back up again. "That's good, because tonight, we're stripping it down." His body heat wrapped around her as he moved to her side, his gaze falling to her lips.

"Stripping it down?"

Taking a piece of her hair, he pulled, wrenching a pleasurable little sting over her scalp. "Baring it all."

Carrie swallowed. "Haven't we already done that?" Not that she was complaining. She'd do it again here, now. Anything he wanted. Levi let her hair slide through his fingers. "No. Not completely." He took her hand, watching her expectantly as he led her toward her bedroom down the hall. He was right; they hadn't bared it all. At least, he hadn't. Sensing that this was something he needed, Carrie remained silent and pliable to his will as he unbuttoned her shirt and slowly peeled it away. Her skirt was next, followed by every other piece of clothing until she was nude in the soft light of the room.

Cool air raced over her skin, but she flushed warm despite it.

"Close your eyes." He stroked her jaw, traced a line down her neck. Carrie complied, taking a small, quick breath as his touch feathered over her collarbone to her shoulder. And then he was stroking both of her arms, his hands touching and caressing the length of her torso, her back, following the dip of her spine to the rise of her ass, leaving no inch untouched and making every nerve come to life. Just as suddenly, the touches stopped, but she didn't open her eyes. The sound of fabric rustling, the sound of his belt opening, and he was guiding her hands until they were palm-down on his chest.

His heart raced beneath her touch, her own answering in kind as he moved in until the soft hair on his chest tickled her breasts. With a soft kiss, he guided her back to the bed until her legs touched against it and he lowered her down, helped her slide back. Carrie opened her eyes to find him kneeling over her, the beautiful lines of his face like a punch in the heart. He moved back and stood, his fingers finding the button of his jeans.

Just like the day they'd gone to the Devil's Kettle, he hesitated. His head tilted a little as if he was asking her if she was ready. She was afraid to respond, didn't want him to interpret any slight movement as unwillingness on her part. She wanted this, needed this part of him. Levi unfastened the button, let the denim gape wide and fall, baring the deeply muscled vee that led down. A muscle in his jaw jumped as he halted the denim's path, his lashes fluttering when he let go and the barrier fell.

She could only stare. Both thighs had been damaged, but the left was the worst. Deep lines gouged through muscle that looked as if it had been modeling dough in a child's hands. Long scars crossed over areas of puckered flesh. Tears burned her eyes, a hot line streaming down her cheek. She couldn't fathom the pain he'd been in, suffering this. An image of him lying in the sand in a pool of blood popped into her mind—how close he'd come to death.

Carrie held her arms out to him, and after a second of hesitation, he knelt on the bed and came to her. She tasted her own tears on his lips when their mouths met. Need flashed hot and demanding, prompting her to pull him closer so she could run her hands everywhere she could reach.

Levi relaxed when she began to explore the map of his injuries, as if her acceptance took a huge weight from him. She drew her fingers along each dip and scar. She hadn't been there to love him through healing, but she was here now to show him that he was as perfect. Carrie wrapped her legs around his and tipped her hips up. She didn't want sweet kisses or foreplay. Just the physical connection that made them whole. Levi found her sweet spot right before he thrust inside, hard, deep, and complete.

In the afterglow, Levi wrapped himself around her and held her close. Carrie settled against him feeling that the final door had closed on the obstacles between them. The path to a relationship was finally fresh, clean, and ready. Instead of a second chance being ready for her, she was ready for it.

Carrie turned in Levi's arms, her heart full. "I'm going to stay."

Chapter Nineteen

Fresh from the shower, body tingling, Carrie nursed her coffee while Levi sat quietly next to her at the kitchen table. She'd worried he'd feel a little awkward this morning after what they'd shared last night, but if he did, he wasn't showing it. If anything, they were like an old married couple with a flirtatious side, sitting easily together while sneaking looks at each other and playing footsie.

When her dad walked in unexpectedly, the slight nausea she'd been fighting off and on since yesterday threatened to make her sick right then and there. If Darren was surprised to see Levi, shirt unbuttoned and hair wet from a shower, looking so comfortable with his arm around the back of Carrie's chair, he didn't show it. Which was odd, because as stoic as cowboys were touted to be, he'd never been shy about holding back what he was thinking.

"Hey, Dad. You're back early," she said with an uncertain smile. "Want some breakfast?" Breakfast which Levi had made not long ago before he'd thrown her back into bed for a morning go-round. Carrie wanted to slide under the table.

She was an adult, sure, but he was still her father, and this was his home. Darren nodded to Levi as he moved to the counter to fill his coffee cup.

"Things all right around here?"

Levi sat straighter and put his forearms on the table. "Yessir." Carrie slid a look from one man to the other. When her father's eyes narrowed and his lips went thin, Levi didn't flinch.

"Seems some things have been getting fixed while I was gone, then."

Levi rose, voice firm but respectful. "That's a conversation for another time, sir."

Darren crossed his arms, carefully gripping his steaming coffee mug. "I say it's a conversation for right damn now."

Visions of a shotgun wedding started to cloud her head. Carrie stood, smoothing her shirt with one hand to try to calm her shaking. Before she could unscramble the images of her dad whipping out a gun and Levi sticking up his hands like a cartoon criminal, Darren went on.

"I'm not a fool. I knew there was a chance the two of you would…reconnect."

Carrie thought about what Levi had said about her father making him promise to leave her behind when he'd left for the military. She realized he'd done what he thought was best at the time. It was a long time ago, but she'd be damned if he was going to step in again. She'd be making her own decisions about her and Levi—about everything.

"I have something to show you." Levi turned and walked out, leaving Carrie to fiddle with the hem of her shirt like she was seventeen again, nervous her dad had learned that she and Levi had just had a romp in the haymow. Because the cool, knowing stare he gave her was the same as it had been then. This time, instead of asking her what she'd been doing to make her look like she'd stolen cookies from a nun, one corner of his lips pulled up into a knowing grin.

"I figured there was more to be said between you two."

Wiping her hands on her jeans, she leaned against the table. "Yes, there was."

He sipped his coffee. "I guess I figured you two might need some closure, if that's what you wanted." Closure implied she and Levi would've said their piece and gone their separate ways. While they'd done the talking thing, something unfinished had turned into so much more.

When Levi came back with a long cardboard tube in his hands, she stopped fidgeting and wondered just what that "more" entailed. He uncapped one end and withdrew rolled paper. Darren and Carrie cleared dishes from the table, and Levi laid the roll down, uncoiling it and holding the edges down with their coffee cups. Her breath caught as the pale blue surface of the paper displayed the sketch and design for a large round barn with an outdoor arena behind it. Pretty bushes and landscaping in the front made a beautiful foundation for a sign, THERAPEUTIC RIDING AND TRAINING CENTER.

Carrie opened her mouth, shut it...opened it again. "This is a therapeutic riding center you mentioned for Paint River." He'd told her about it during one of their late-night conversations. Levi splayed his hands on the bottom of the print, the seriousness in his demeanor cracking a bit as the corners of his eyes crinkled. "We want you to have it. As a joint venture, benefiting both ranches, but more importantly, the patients who need the services that would be provided. I've had a long conversation with the company wanting to expand here, and they'd like to come to Agate Falls and take a look."

She put a hand to her chest, dumbfounded. "Wait, what about the campground?"

"No campground." He moved to her side and kissed her hair. "This center will be profitable and can be constructed without changing much of the ranch."

Darren drained his cup, eyeing the prints. "With all

respect, Levi, how far do we take this thing?"

"The therapy center in no way integrates tourism the way we've set it up at Paint River. You provide the space for the center, and we'll offer temporary housing for clients at Paint River with a shuttle that goes back and forth between the ranches."

Levi went into specifics on how the arrangement worked, but Carrie's thoughts were straying to other possibilities. She could possibly offer treatments as well, right on-site, so the patients who came for therapeutic riding could also have massages to relax muscles and reduce pain. She could work right here, on the property she knew best. If the time came that her vision worsened to the point she couldn't drive, there was no worry about leaving home to go to work.

The men kept on talking, but she didn't process anything beyond the fact that Levi was committing to this; that he'd said he loved her, had bared his injuries to her. Elation could have lifted her to the moon in that moment. Levi was her other half. Had always been, and fate was eagerly intervening this time around.

"Show me the exact location outside where you want to put it," her dad said. The men crossed to the door and Carrie snagged Levi's arm, pulling him back.

"I don't know what to say."

Mindless of her dad waiting by the door, Levi kissed her fully, softly. Pulling back, he ran his thumbs down the sides of her face. "Saying you love me will suffice."

She hugged him tight. "I love you." Her dad made a nondescript sound behind them. She stepped back, and Levi gave a nod before turning away. They walked out, and she heard the sound of a car door shut. Carrie poured herself coffee, her mind spinning, sending a wave of light-headedness. The nausea came back, rising bitterly into her throat. She drank some water and searched for a Tums.

There was so much to take in, to plan, to talk about. She

didn't have time to be getting sick.

Was she hoping too much? It was all coming together, creating a pretty picture of what could be. There were still so many what-ifs, so many things that might not work.

"Carrie?"

She spun to the sound of her name. Rylan stood in the doorway, one hand gripping her hip, the other propped on the door. Fatigue and pain clouded her face. Carrie set down her cup and rushed over. "Rylan! What is it?" She helped her inside, but Rylan waved an annoyed hand and shook her head.

"It's this baby! It's ripping my spine apart, I swear. I hate to just show up, but I was hoping…well, Levi said that you were a master at massages and—"

"Of course," Carrie interjected. "I'm happy to help. Here." She spun a kitchen chair around and helped Rylan straddle it. Grabbing two fluffy kitchen towels, Carrie placed them over the back of the chair so Ry could cross her arms over them comfortably and lean forward.

"Oooh, see, this feels better already."

Carrie washed and warmed her hands under the tap and downed an antacid to push back another burn in her chest. She soaked a clean rag in hot water and wrung it out, making a mental note to finish her mostly untouched breakfast when she was done. Nothing had tasted good the past few days, and the heartburn had killed her appetite.

"You with me?" she teased, giving Rylan a nudge. A groan was her response, followed by a yawn. "Can't sleep because my hips and lower back hurt so much. If I toss too much, I wake up Cole. Hell, if I try to sleep on the couch, he wakes up and fusses after me." There was a lot of affection in the frustration-laced words. "That man and his constant fussing. I love him, but I need him to go away."

Carrie grinned and reached to move Rylan's hair out of the way, but stopped, trying to figure out if it was in a knotted ponytail or a braid gone horribly wrong. Pulling the rubber band loose, she ran her fingers through the long strands and straightened it the best she could. Poor Rylan. Hot, pregnant mess.

"I always heard first babies are the worst," she commented and began braiding.

"This is my second baby."

Carrie paused, realizing how much she really didn't know Rylan. They'd only met a couple of times, and aside from the trip to the day spa, hadn't spent much time together. Still, she felt comfortable around her as if they'd known each other a lot longer. Sophie, too.

"I had a daughter. Rachel." Rylan's voice went heavy with affection. "She passed when she was a toddler, in a car accident."

Carrie slowed the braiding process, her hands suddenly cold. "Oh, Ry, I can't imagine." Funny how you could wallow in your own self-pity now and again, but someone else always had it worse.

"Losing her is what brought me to Paint River. See, the thing is about this place, this beautiful land...it has a way of taking you in when you're broken and putting you back together."

Carrie finished the braid and put it over Rylan's shoulder, then rubbed her hands together to warm her palms as she pondered her friend's words.

"Sophie, too. She came here not knowing which end was up, and in the end, she figured it out."

"And caught Tucker in the process." A crazy miracle, that. He'd always been a player with a heart of gold, but she was still surprised to see that wild man had been caught and tied down.

Rylan laughed. "Yeah. Well, neither of them had a choice, I don't think. Kind of like Cole and me. I knew from the moment I met him that he was going to be trouble...and mine." As Carrie massaged her shoulders, Rylan relayed how she'd met Cole in a bar after getting off a Greyhound bus in the wrong town. It had been a coincidence that he'd been exactly the man she'd been looking for to take her to Paint River Ranch—her boss, as it turned out—and the one she'd butt heads with until they both stopped fighting their attraction for each other.

"I was afraid," Rylan said tiredly. "When I met Birdie, I was scared I wouldn't be able to be a mother to her after losing my own child. That fear took a toll on Cole and me."

Working a knot from the middle of Rylan's back, Carrie nodded. "That had to be incredibly hard."

"It was. Fear, it can keep you from what you need. I almost lost Cole and Birdie both before I figured out that I just needed to stop being scared."

"How?" How could anyone get over fear like that? What Rylan had faced was something from a movie. Extreme, unreal. By comparison, her own fears seemed small.

"I guess I just decided I wanted Cole and Birdie more than I wanted to be afraid. What purpose was that fear serving me? I knew I loved Cole almost right away. I wanted him more than I wanted to hang on to the fear." She groaned as Carrie applied firm pressure to her lower back. "That's sooo goood."

"Your poor back. I'm going to manipulate your hips a little, so just relax." By the time she was done, Rylan was like a puddle in the chair, but her breathing had become even and smooth, her back relaxed in a way that Carrie hoped would ease the pain for a lasting period of time. She rewet the warm towel and placed it on her friend's lower back under her shirt.

"Better?"

"God, so much better. Thank you so much."

"Anytime. I wish you'd come to me sooner. I'm sorry I didn't offer in case you needed me."

Rylan waved her off, her cheek resting on her crossed

arms, eyes closed. "You want to know a secret?"

"Sure."

"I accidentally found out the baby's gender at my ultrasound the other day. I promised Cole I wouldn't find out. I'm dying to tell someone and I can't trust Sophie to keep her mouth shut."

"No! Really?"

Even though they were alone, Rylan waved her to come closer, and Carrie bent so she could whisper in her ear.

"Congratulations!"

A knock sounded on the screen door, a deep voice startling them both. "Congratulations, what?"

"Jesus, Cole." Rylan sighed. "Did you come looking for me?" Her eye roll was both annoyed and loving. He stepped inside, closing the door gently behind him. Hat in his hands, he nodded to Carrie, who had a hard time keeping the grin off her face. Protective cowboy to a T. Rylan glanced at her and made a, "shhhh, don't tell," face.

"I was worried. Sophie said you'd mentioned coming by, so I figured I'd better check on you." He helped his wife from the chair and she leaned against him. For all her angst over his protectiveness, she held on to him like he was her lifeline, her voice tender when they spoke softly to each other. Carrie's throat tightened a little as she called good-bye to them and stood in the kitchen, a hand over her heart and the other on the back of the chair.

Rylan had all that love and her pieces put back together because she'd stopped being afraid. Levi was offering her the same. A chance at love, at a family and reconnection with her roots. She'd been right to take this chance. Grabbing a piece of toast from her plate, she munched on it as she went upstairs to get the things she'd gathered from the attic the other day, including a wedding gift for Maeve.

For the first time in too long, she was calm. Her life had promise. Everything was going to be okay.

Chapter Twenty

Levi took the porch steps two at a time, pulling his cell from his back pocket to check messages before pushing the door open. The scent of coffee and bacon still hung in the air, though breakfast had been hours ago. Still welcoming, the scents made his stomach rumble. For the past two days, he and Darren had been going nonstop, talking about locations to put the riding center, taking measurements, running quick errands. Elated with the possibilities this brought to Agate Falls, Levi was glad the project had fallen into his lap after all.

Things in general were coming together. A year ago, he'd barely been able to stand or maneuver stairs or sleep without nightmares clawing at him. Now, at the brink of every morning, he woke next to the only woman he'd ever love, in a place where he was making a difference, looking forward to the hard work that fed his soul.

"Carrie?" He and Darren needed to ride out to the lower pasture to discuss which cattle were best to take back to the Colorado market, and they only had a few hours of daylight left. He wanted to be sure she knew before they left. Clearing the kitchen, Levi checked the living room and Carrie's room. Her coat and boots were still in the entryway, the house silent.

Checking the rest of the lower level, he went to the staircase, listening for any sound before calling up. "Carrie?"

Not waiting for an answer, he trotted upstairs, chastising himself for being worried. She'd probably gone outside and found something to fiddle with. She wasn't in the upper level, though a rag and some cleaning solution said she'd been there at some time. Levi turned to go back down but stopped, remembering she'd talked the other day about sorting through boxes in the attic. Going to the narrow staircase that lead one more level up, he found the attic door half open.

Dust settled through rays of sunlight coming in from the dormer windows as he navigated the narrow, cluttered space. "Carrie?" A few boxes were open, their contents set aside, and wads of newspaper dotted the floor. He fingered a small figurine of a red bird, next to it, an envelope-size frame holding a matching cardinal cut from colored glass.

With a grin, he recalled how Carrie had spent hours creating patterns and cutting glass, working meticulously to piece them together. He'd often sit next to her, watching, telling her about the day, prolonging having to leave to get back to Paint River. Rubbing a thumb over the fine layer of dust on the stained glass, he looked down and his heart lurched to his throat.

Behind a wad of paper on the floor, he spied a pale length of arm. Bending, he moved the papers, finding Carrie lying on her side, hidden by the boxes.

"Jesus, Carrie!" Smoothing hair from her face, he found the strands damp, her face clammy, pale and slick with sweat. He gently turned her onto her back, her body limp and clothes damp. Frantically, he searched for a pulse at her neck, watching for the rise and fall of her chest...sure she wasn't breathing where there was no sign of movement.

A flutter beneath his fingers, her pulse slow but present, and the very faint swell of her chest allowed him to exhale in relief. No doctor needed to tell him her blood sugar had crashed; Levi had seen this happen to her before. She used to keep little packets of sugar gel in the bathroom. Levi was reluctant to leave her, even for a moment. Reassuring himself with one more rise and fall of her chest, he darted from the attic and slid down the stairs as he pulled out his phone to call Sophie.

It rang twice…four times, five to his combination of cussing and prayer, before the line connected.

"Hey, Lev—"

"Bring your medical kit to Agate Falls. Upstairs in the attic. It's Carrie."

Accidentally dropping the phone, it went sliding down the hall as he jumped down the last few stairs. He didn't bother to grab it, but hurried to the bathroom and rummaged around for the gel. God, it had been years since he'd been through this with her. Who the hell knew where she kept the sugar stuff anymore, or if that was even what he was supposed to use.

What if things had changed and she needed something else? He'd never bothered to ask her—they hadn't had a frank conversation about her health beyond what she'd told him. He'd been too busy trying to reassure her that he could handle it, that they could handle it. Her fragile blood sugar and the possibility of failing eyesight weren't little obstacles; they were huge, lifelong battles.

Rummaging through a drawer, he found two packets of the gel, gripped them like precious treasure, and raced back up the stairs. He'd been to battle, twice. Two full tours, months of simulated training. Then he'd come home and battled his own body for his freedom, his life. Nothing had held him down then—not an insurgent's bomb, not his own weakness. Sliding to his knees beside her, Levi cradled Carrie's head in his hand and set her up on his lap. He'd fight for her just as much.

Ripping open the packet, he leaned low over her. "Nothing will stop us, Sunshine. Do you hear me?" He pinched her lips open, conflicted if he should actually give her any considering she was unconscious. The times he'd given it to her before, she'd been going downhill, but was still awake. Her brain needed sugar, and the only way he could get it into her until Sophie arrived was the gel.

It was just goo, and he'd go slow...squeezing a bit from the top, he administered it into her mouth, setting his jaw. Thinking back over the morning, he tried to pinpoint a warning that this was going to happen. She'd been a little flushed, but he'd thought that was from the excitement of the therapy center. She hadn't eaten much, though maybe she had later when he'd gone outside.

"Levi!"

"In here!"

The clomping of double footsteps filled the air. Sophie came into view, followed by Darren, whose eyes went huge and flashed something Levi couldn't read.

"How long has she been down?" Sophie grabbed a small kit and began pulling things out. Grabbing Carrie's finger, she poked with a small needle. A well of blood glistened as she placed it on a monitor.

"I don't know. I just found her right before I called you. Darren and I were outside—"

"When is the last time you saw her awake?"

Levi caught Darren's eyes and shrugged. "Four hours or so ago." It hurt to admit it. Had she been this way for four goddamned hours? What if he hadn't come in to see her and had just gone to the fields like he and Darren planned? They'd have been gone another two, maybe three hours. She wouldn't have been able to hold out that long…

Sophie fired off another round of questions as she set up an intravenous kit. He recognized the setup similar to what he'd seen on base—a bag of fluid, tubing, a glass tube that read "Dextrose" on it. Carrie didn't flinch or make a sound as Sophie started an IV, a moment later pushing medication from the tube into it.

"I called the first responders just in case," Sophie muttered, her eyes searching Carrie's face. Levi stroked her hair, glancing at Darren from the corner of his eye. The older man had his arms crossed, a thumb on his lower lip and a familiar worry in his expression. No matter how many times he'd been through this with his daughter, it was apparent the apprehension didn't ever go away.

Movement in his lap, the slide of hair against his jeans. Carrie opened her eyes, closed them right away. Elation burst through him. "Hey, Sunshine, come on. Open your eyes."

"Hey," she mumbled, yawning like she was waking up from an ordinary nap. "Are we in the attic?" She glanced around slowly. "Sophie?"

"Welcome back."

Carrie raised her arm and groaned at the IV. "No… really?" Levi helped her sit, then stripped out of his flannel shirt and used it to wipe her forehead. "How long was I out?" The question was aimed at him and he winced. He hadn't been here. Unable to speak around the guilt clogging his throat, he just shrugged. More footfalls on the steps, unfamiliar voices that blended with Sophie's soft tone. He figured the first responder crew was here, but he was too focused on Carrie to care. When she mouthed, "I'm sorry," he drew her into a gentle embrace and wanted to punch himself. She didn't have anything to be sorry about.

Sophie turned to him. "We're just going to check her over better, okay?"

The first responders crammed into the small space, leaving Levi to reluctantly back out. He crossed his arms and waited as close to Carrie as he could, legs wide, neck tense, watching. Darren joined him, gave him a small slap on the shoulder.

"Good thing you came in when you did." The older man's voice was weary. He turned and faced Levi, their shoulders touching as Darren leaned closer to Levi's ear. "You prepared to handle this, son? Because if you ask her to stay…" His voice trailed off. Levi kept an eye on Carrie, working his jaw from left to right. He'd taken charge of operative and night missions, and none of them frightened him as much as one small, unpredictable woman.

"I am."

Darren grunted but said nothing else. Finally, Sophie helped Carrie up and came toward the door. She brushed herself off, insisting she was fine, yet as he came forward to take her hand, she moved away and didn't look at him. Sophie took her arm, and they spoke softly together as they went slowly down the stairs, a trail of people behind. Levi waited until last, losing sight of her as she rounded the landing and kept going down.

At the bottom, there was a flurry of paperwork, more questions, and a lot of Carrie insisting she didn't need to go to the hospital. The crew finally left and Levi found himself in awkward silence, though he didn't know why. Carrie went into her room, diverting her eyes as she disappeared inside. Confused and worried, he moved to follow, but Darren stepped in his way.

"I'd like a bit with my daughter."

Levi moved back as the older man went inside and shut the door.

"What the hell is going on?" he asked more to himself, though Sophie patted his shoulder and made a sympathetic sound.

"Give her a minute. It's scary when this happens to someone, you know? She mentioned she's had an upset stomach and hadn't eaten enough lately. You're going to feed her, let her get some rest, and keep an eye on her sugars tonight. Okay?"

Grateful that Sophie was there, Levi gave her a quick hug and walked her out to her car. Back inside, he tried to make coffee but found himself pacing instead. A half an hour turned into one. Then another half. The more time ticked, the more the need to see Carrie built. The pressure peaked, and he grabbed his jacket, intending to go out and find something to kick around. The bedroom door opened.

"She okay?" he asked as Darren came out.

"Sleeping. You go ahead home, son." Home? Right. No. He was home with one foot on Agate Falls and the other on Paint River. Whichever side Carrie was on was where he'd hang his hat.

"I'll wait." He pulled out a kitchen chair, but Darren put a hand on the back.

"I said go on home." The ice in the older man's tone brought a heavy dose of stubborn fight in him. Getting the impression he'd done something wrong, Levi put his hand next to the other man's on the back of the chair and bent a bit so he was eye level.

"I respect the hell out of you, Darren, but I need to know what this attitude is about. Tell me, straight up, what is it?"

Darren's nostrils flared, the lines around his mouth and between his eyes going deep and making his skin appear older, more weathered. In one blink, Levi saw how worry aged him and cut straight to the bone.

"My girl's going to lose her sight. Did you know that?"

Ah, hell, she'd told him. An ache went through his left thigh, making him want to sit, but he stood steady. He knew she'd been waiting for the right time to confide in her father, if there ever was a good time for bad news. With a singular nod, Levi straightened and ran a hand over his face. "I knew."

"And yet you've been giving her the deluded impression that she can live here? Out here, miles from anything, and be safe?"

"She wants to stay." She'd been confident in that decision. But despite what they both wanted, maybe they hadn't looked at the big picture clearly enough. Sophie had been around today, luckily. What if she was gone, and the first responders were busy doing something else? A slim possibility, but something he needed to consider. He wouldn't be around all the time, either. Realistically, he'd be gone as long as the task at hand required—Darren, too. Running a hand through his hair, Levi tried to dismiss a rising amount of doubt. He'd asked her to stay first, pushed the issue a bit because he'd been selfish. He couldn't imagine life without her again. But even if it cost her?

Darren crossed to the counter and put his hands on it, leaned low. "She did want to stay." He made a half turn, and Levi's stomach bottomed out. "She's changed her mind. Carrie wants to go back to Wyoming."

"She wants that, or *you* do?" He spit out the words before he thought it through. Three steps and he was at the older man's side. They reached for each other at the same time, clasping forearms in a lock of pigheaded will and love for the same woman.

"I do. I want it." The small, soft voice made them both spin. Carrie hugged herself inside a sweater, her face pale and drawn. Levi was hit with the sensation that he'd just lost a war he thought he'd already won.

• • •

She *was* fragile, sometimes. As her dad ducked his head and walked out, Carrie imagined she was like the stained glass panel, mended here and there, but with new, ultrafine cracks along the surface that threatened to cut through. She was strong, but easily chipped, and the final shatter was always a guessing game.

She was thankful for so many things that he'd brought into her life in these past two weeks. When she'd opened her eyes and awareness had seeped in that she was on the ground, her head in Levi's lap, the first punch of panic had come. But then she'd looked up into his face and the absolute devastation in his expression had consumed her with fear and grief.

Love might be strong and steadfast, but she couldn't expect this of him. The unpredictability, the constant wondering when the next crack was going to happen. She'd settled into a safe, comfortable life in Wyoming for a reason. When she was at work, she was surrounded by people. At home, someone was usually there, and if not, a neighbor was always checking in. As things progressed, she'd need even more help. Babysitting wasn't part of the deal, at least not for a cowboy with two ranches to work.

How could she expect him not to turn resentful of the care she'd need—hell, needed now—and the struggles her disability would bring? He might love her, but she couldn't ask this of him. And she couldn't stop the fear.

"Talk to me." Levi put one big hand on the table as if he was holding himself back. She leaned against the arch between the kitchen and living room and pulled the sweater tighter. The only way to get through this was to face it head-on. No more dreaming about things she couldn't have.

"I'm going back to Wyoming."

His face was strained, the creases across his forehead and around his eyes deep. This was the man who'd been to war, not once but twice. Who'd seen death and felt terror and had been subjected to soul-deep trauma. And here she was, causing him more pain by trying to save him the trouble of her.

"I'm sorry," she uttered softly when he didn't reply.

The line of his jaw jumped a few times before he wet his lower lip and spread his hands wide. "I don't want you to go. That should be obvious. The whole 'I love you' thing and all that." The bitterness in his voice hurt, but she didn't expect any less.

"We have history, Levi."

"Yes, we do."

"And history repeats itself, right? You went away, and left me behind because of my health. And then I went away because of my health. And here we are, right back where we started and it's already gone wrong." She wanted to run her hands through his messy hair and follow the strands with her fingers. Pull him close and inhale deeply of the fresh air and warmth that always followed him—commit every line and sound and taste of him to memory.

"This is going to keep happening to me, Levi. Like it always has. And...I'm scared. Of what it will mean for us, down the line."

He slapped the table, tipping his head to the side like he was trying to truly understand. "Of course it is. It will. You think I don't know that? God, Carrie, I'm here to help you. To be *with you*, no matter what." He advanced on her, taking her face between his hands. "Do you think my family gave up on me when I was broken? Of course not. Why do you think I'm still here?"

His scent and warmth gave her a rush of strength and peace stronger than any medicine. It would be easy to believe him, if she could get past the continual replay of worry. What if he hadn't come inside the house when he had? It was a sickening revolution of "what if?" that refused to stop. Those two words had been engrained in her since she was small, and she couldn't just make them go away.

"I don't know how to not be afraid, Levi." It was a constant storm inside her, always rain. "As much as I love you, that's not something you can help me with."

"Leaving me is your answer then?" His stony voice razed her to the bone.

"I don't have an answer. I'm just doing what's familiar and safe until I figure it out."

He looked up to the ceiling, his shoulders and back relaxing as if the anger were melting away. "Then you should go. You're right, you *should* go."

She sagged a bit against the wall, tears flashing into her eyes, but she wouldn't let them run. The less they hashed this out, the better, before she changed her mind and saddled him with a life he'd come to regret. She wouldn't be able to bear it if he grew to resent her.

Levi cleared his throat. "It was a mistake to think this would work."

"Levi—"

"Does it make it easier for you when I say that?"

Tears fell. This had to end, right now. "Please go." He reached for her, one light grip bringing her to his chest, his lips on hers with a soft, lasting demand, wrenching her heart.

He jerked away from her and strode to the door and walked out, slamming it. His retreating form was a blur, the pain in her chest double what it had been the last time he'd walked out. This time, she had asked him to.

Chapter Twenty-One

He'd always been a risk-taker. As a kid, he'd gone head-to-head with things his brothers shied away from, like free-climbing in the lower peaks of Blue Head Mountain not far from the ranch. A little powder for his hands, shoes with a good sole, some rope to rappel down with, and a lot of determination was all he needed. He'd dig his fingers and toes into crevices in the mountain face and pull himself up, scaling high. Sometimes, the rock had been smooth and offered little grip, but he'd keep searching until he found a hold, and he wouldn't quit until he'd reached the top.

Never once had he looked down.

He'd left for the military, knowing full well there was a war going on and he was taking a chance with his life. But he'd gone for the experience, with his head held high, and never looked back. Now, he'd taken a risk with Carrie. No safety nets, no regrets. Just him and her and the love he had coursing through him like fire. She'd pushed him off the cliff and he was falling in his first free fall.

There wasn't anything to grab on to, to slow him down.

Fear had gotten the better of both of them. The clock on his nightstand flipped to 2:00 a.m. A day plus some separated now from the moment she'd asked him to leave. He'd resolved to give her some time to rest, maybe think—change her mind, if he was lucky. Darren probably wouldn't let him within ten feet of her at the moment, too afraid Levi would try to change her mind again—to take a risk.

How could he ask that of her and keep a clear conscience? Her life in Wyoming was set the way it was for a reason: security. He could offer her money, stability, love. But he couldn't take the risk away, and he couldn't ask her to take chances she didn't want.

Frustrated, Levi stood from the edge of his bed and walked through the room. In fourteen hours, his mother would be getting married. He'd worked with Cole and Tucker all day, getting things ready. What a bittersweet kick in the ass that was going to be. Her marriage to their father had been a loveless one, born of duty, mostly. After Cooper Haywood's death three years ago, his mom was free to reconnect with Jim Guilfoyle, whom she'd secretly loved for years. Tomorrow, she was going to marry the man she thought she'd never have.

A genuine pang of happiness touched his heart. His mother deserved this joy, and it was his honor to walk her down the aisle tomorrow and give her away to her best friend. Even if it was going to be hard to keep self-pity out of it.

Levi yanked the bedroom door open. The hallway was dark, the house quiet when he paused to listen. It was just him, his ma, and his niece Birdie, who liked to spend the night every now and then. They were at the other end of the house, which would make them oblivious to his being up at this hour.

Still in the jeans he'd worked in all day, Levi padded the hallway to the basement staircase, needing to ease off some of the tension. He'd go into the gym and force his legs to carry him through a beating on the treadmill. And then he'd sulk through the pain that followed, letting it clog his brain. After that, he had a date with a bottle of Jack. No peppers.

Cracking his neck from side to side, he trotted down and went into the bedroom that had been converted into a workout room. His iPod lay draped over the treadmill from the last time he'd forced himself through a run. Putting in his earphones, he cranked up Macklemore and started the machine.

Ten minutes into it, his thighs were aching but he ignored it. He'd fought long and hard to be able to stand up and walk on his own. Damn it, he was going to run as far and as fast as he fucking wanted to. Punishment? Sure. Bring it. He was a marine, and one who was good at being numb. Right now, he needed numbness to help him forget there was a woman a mile away who was once again out of reach.

The pain jacked higher, ripping through his left leg and making him stumble. Levi grabbed the bar and steadied himself, grunting with the exertion it took to find his rhythm again. Completely numb now, his mind began to drift. A familiar pattern of patchwork desert tan and brown. So much neutral with barely definable lines to separate the horizon from the ground. Even the sky was tan some days, hidden by hazy clouds the color of the sand.

He was a shape in a colorless world, until he looked down and saw the stripes of red soaking into the sand. Stark, brilliant, and beautiful in a way of color over monotony, the crimson drew his eyes as it turned to a deep purple and then a muddy shade of brown. Levi shook his head to fight the memory. He recalled the night he'd been blown up less and less now, but when it did happen, one thing always stood out: brown eyes looking down at him as his body pulsed more crimson into the dirt.

Eyes that crinkled at the corners, and long, dark lashes

that framed the perfect almond shape of each. He'd imagined those eyes for years, months. It was the essence of her that came through.

Sweat dripping down his forehead, Levi grabbed the rail again as his legs began to shake. How long had he run this time? He'd lost count, not that it mattered. Some of the tension had lessened inside him, though it was there, ready to make a swift comeback if he didn't control it. Wiping his hand on his pants, he turned down the machine, grappling to get a good breath through the pain slicing his legs. He ran the hem of his T-shirt over his face and pulled the headphones from his ears.

He made it to the bathroom for a drink, then unsteadily forced himself back to the stairway where he plopped down on the third step up. Doubled over, he breathed through the agony.

I'm not fragile. He recalled Carrie's words and wished they were true. She was fragile, sometimes. So was he, like now, when his body was riddled with pain and he couldn't do anything but wait it out. They could find a way to cushion each other in times when strength was hard to find. There had to be a way.

He stood, suddenly tired. His left knee buckled under his body weight. Levi grabbed the stair rail and found his center. He hated when his twenty-six-year-old body acted like it was ninety. One foot on each step, he closed his eyes. He went up one more, kept his feet braced with one on each rise, never allowing them to meet on the same step. A bead of sweat ran down his temple. Carrie's face had been slick with sweat, her skin pale and clammy. He'd never felt skin that cold on a live person.

This is going to keep happening to me.

Levi put a hand on his knee and leaned low to catch his breath. Why did it have to hurt so badly? Rising up with a tight sigh, he wiped sweat from his face and eyed the railing. Screw it, he needed to sit, just for a minute.

He sat and hung his head, concentrating on his breathing. Hating himself for being weak…for not having answers.

"Uncle Levi?" The timid voice cut through his head. "Are you hurt?"

Birdie. At the very top, feet crossed, one little hand on the rail as she peered down at him.

He tried to smile. "A little bit, honey. But don't tell Grandma. I'll be okay."

A soft shuffle from above. "I need help." The sweetness of her voice gave him goose bumps. He hung his head over his knees again, just for a second. Everything was fine, going back to normal. The pain was almost gone. "Daddy told me I wasn't allowed to wake up Grandma unless there was a 'mergency."

"Are *you* hurt?" His pulse started to slow, his skin cooling.

"No." Another soft sliding noise, as if she were on her butt and coming down the stairs one by one. A shiver went over him. *No, sweetheart, no.* It was bad enough she was seeing him like this, battered and weak; he didn't need her up close and personal.

"What's wrong?" The lump in his throat made it hard to talk. That and the intermittent zaps of pain-filled electricity running along his leg.

"I lost a tooth." One final thump and he was awash in the smell of fruity shampoo and freshly washed kid. That he was spent and limp and sweating like a pig didn't faze her a bit; one little hand popped into his view with a tiny tooth in the middle of her palm. "See?"

Birdie's feet were crossed right next to his shoulder, the fluff of her neon pink tutu with silver glitter on the hem sticking straight up. He reached over and picked up the tooth, giving her what he hoped was a grin.

"That's a fine tooth."

"Why are you sittin' on the stairs?"

Good question. "Because I'm tired," he said. She moved closer, the fluff tickling his face as she stood. And then her warm hand was gripping his left one, the embrace of her fingers strong for such a tiny girl.

"I'll help you. Come on."

The lump in his throat worked its way down the very center of his chest. Birdie tenderly patted his hand. "Come on," she said again, as if encouraging a reluctant puppy. She paused a minute, then leaned closer. "If you're not ready, I'll wait."

"Why?" The question burst out of him. It was the middle of the night, and he was on the bottom, feeling sorry for himself. Here she was, all pink and little and cute, with her hand holding on to his as if she could singularly bring him up.

"Because I love you."

Levi gripped Birdie's hand gently, trying and failing to hold back the sob-like sound that came out of him. She tilted her head, brow furrowed. "Daddy waited for you. Grandma, too. And Uncle Tuck."

"They did?" Yeah, they had. He knew. The times he'd had leave, but hadn't come home, too scared he'd be a deserter and stay put. When he'd been broken and cursing at everyone and hating himself while his body healed, they'd waited.

"When you were in the army."

He gave a fake cringe. "Marines."

Birdie giggled. "Daddy says love is patient." She fluffed her skirt. Levi's brows knit together; he was at a loss as to what to say. A few minutes ago, he'd been drowning in discomfort and pity, and now he was getting words of wisdom from a six-year-old with one front tooth. "When did you get so smart, Birdie?"

She shrugged, but a smug smile curved her pink lips. "Daddy had to wait for Rylan. He loved her a lot before."

Levi handed her back her tooth. "Before what?"

She frowned at him as if he should know. "Before she said yes!"

Cole was the most impatient person Levi knew. It was hard to imagine him waiting on a woman. Rylan had been through a lot before she came to Paint River to work as a housekeeper. He recalled Cole telling him about it—how she'd lost her daughter in an accident and didn't have it in her to take on a new family.

So Cole had waited her out. With that big, stubborn heart of his, Cole probably did anything in his power to convince her—even if he didn't have all the answers.

Birdie pulled on his sleeve. "I need you to put my tooth under my pillow for the tooth fairy. Come on."

With a groan, he got up, feeling an ache in every muscle along his chest and back and thighs, but it didn't hurt anymore. She guided him like he was a baby learning to walk. It was cute, enduring, and sweet as anything, and he'd needed this break from his emotions. Hand in hand, they went up, the swish of her skirt brushing against his leg as she rambled on about her chicken named Fred Bologna.

She was as patient as could be, yakking his ear off, tugging him along. He may have gone slower just to prolong the moment.

"We made it," Levi huffed as they reached the top and crossed to the living room. Mentally and physically worn, he laid on his back on the hardwood floor, too worn to drag himself to the couch, arms outstretched as coolness from the wood seeped through his shirt.

"Birdie, grab two pillows off the couch, okay?"

He heard her little feet as she scrambled to do what he'd asked. And then softness was under his head and he told

Birdie to lie down next to him and put her tooth under her pillow. And his breathing evened out to the sound of crickets coming in from outside. The patter of light rain on the roof started a bit later. Birdie's little body was snug against his side, her breathing slow and even.

He reached into his pocket and dug around for the twenty-dollar bill he'd put in there earlier, and carefully replaced the tooth with it. He grinned a bit. Cole would have a fit at the precedent the tooth fairy had just set. Birdie deserved it and more, because she'd just shown him that it didn't matter if you were physically strong. It was the strength of the heart, and the love inside it, that counted.

Levi let himself drift off again, to the smell of bubblegum shampoo and the warmth of his little niece, comforting and strong, next to him. He absorbed the lazy sound of dying rain as his mind slipped into a hazy state. He saw the patchwork of beige and tan again, his memory slipping back to that place… that day that had wounded him.

He'd daydreamed about going back to Carrie. When he'd been lost, walking a line between military man and cowboy, he'd think of Carrie and it would become clear. He had Paint River dirt ingrained in his skin, deeply, to the bone, and love for one beautiful woman cycling through his heart. He'd never be free of her, never wanted to be. She'd been there as deeply inside him as the ranch, and in every daydream, he found his way back to her.

Even as he lay in the sand, staring at the star-studded sky, his body bleeding into the hot, packed sand beneath him. He'd seen her eyes in the stars, imagined her voice telling him to hold on. His brain had concocted all of it, of course, but even thinking of it now gave him a chill. She'd been his angel. He'd remembered that he had to get back to her. It had driven him to find the strength to flip onto his stomach, nearly biting through the flesh on his forearm to keep from screaming through the pain. As he began to pull himself forward with his arms, useless legs dragging behind, each inch ripping through him like razor-sharp teeth, he'd clung to her—he had to make it home.

A recon unit had intercepted him. He couldn't remember feeling relief—his last memory of that night was grabbing the front of a medic's uniform and pulling him closer. "Tell Carrie I'm comin' home."

She'd had so much impact on his life…how could he give up now?

Love waits. He'd wait for *her* this time.

Careful not to disturb Birdie, Levi sat and pushed to his feet. Carrie loved him; he knew she did. They didn't have answers today, but he wasn't going to give up. He'd wait, and if he could find the right words, maybe she'd wait, too.

Going into his office, he rummaged around in the papers scattered across his desk. He had an email printed somewhere from the therapy center that Darren needed to see. Maybe bringing him business stuff would keep the elder rancher busy long enough that Levi could have some time with Carrie.

Finding the packet for the therapy center, he pulled out the stack of papers, flipping through them to see if the email was inside. A small pamphlet plopped out, upside down. Ignoring it, he continued…until the word "diabetic" caught his attention. Glancing at the pamphlet, he dropped the other papers and picked it up. Heart racing, he opened it and scanned the information inside.

No. Shit.

He read it again, slowly, cover to cover, and then picked up the phone. Four in the morning or not, he'd leave a message and call again if he didn't hear back by breakfast. This couldn't wait.

Chapter Twenty-Two

"You're sure about this?"

"I'm fine. My sugar is good and I feel great, Dad. It's a good time."

Forty-eight hours had passed since she'd had the low, but her body had recovered and she felt more energetic than she had in days. Plus, the weather was great with just enough cloud cover to make the four-hour drive easier on her eyes. She tried not to think that this might be the last time she drove herself to and from Agate Falls, and truthfully, she had no idea how long it would take until she was ready to come back. The longer she delayed leaving, the harder it would be.

"You don't want to stay for the wedding?" Her dad's face was heavy with worry and she hated making him feel that way. Shaking her head, she pulled away and glanced at her bags sitting near the kitchen door.

"I can't, Dad." She always missed this place for days after a visit. Sometimes the longing was so bad, it seemed like she was leaving home for the first time all over again. Her heart was here, even if she couldn't be physically, and despite the heartache, she was grateful to have had more time here, and with Levi. Unexpected, but so damn sweet, their reunion had taken her through the gamut of emotions. What they'd shared was rich and real, and a testament to the connection people make over time, even if it's not meant for long.

It couldn't be more, not when she was this afraid. Her body was unpredictable and all the love in the world couldn't change that. Her father made a deep, grumbly sound as if he'd been debating with himself and somehow lost. "I just wish things could be different for you."

Her face went tingly, her eyes and nose starting to sting. Holding back tears, she swallowed hard and nodded. "Me, too."

"What about Levi?"

The question stunned her a bit. "What about him?"

"Look, Carrie," he said, looking to the ground. "I know I was pretty hard on him about you staying. I shouldn't have been. Levi—"

"Dad—"

"Levi is a good man. I don't doubt there's nothing that boy wouldn't do to help you stay here. If it's what you wanted."

Looping an arm around her dad's neck, she hugged him again, needing the physical contact but also hoping it would end the conversation. She didn't have it in her to go there anymore.

"You give Maeve and Jim my love. The little stained glass piece I found for them is wrapped up on the living room table." With that, she moved to grab her bags; he beat her to it and walked out to her truck, seeming resigned. Going around to the passenger side, he put her bags in the front seat, then checked his watch. "Not quite noon. You'll get home by suppertime."

"I'll call as soon as I get there." She opened the door but lacked enthusiasm about getting in. Putting on her sunglasses,

Carrie pushed down the heaviness inside her. A part of her wanted to say good-bye to Levi, but after what she'd said to him, it was probably best not to. Why prolong a fantasy that would never be real? Kicking the gravel at her feet, she hitched a thumb toward the house. "You better go wash up for that wedding."

Darren shut the passenger door and tipped his hat as he came around. "Love you, girlie," he called as he headed to the house, leaving her standing there to absorb the sounds and take in the air and one last view. She was just about to slip into the truck when the sound of racing tires over spitting gravel pulled her attention. Levi's truck barreled down the drive and came to a sliding halt beside hers. He'd barely parked before jumping out. He wore a white dress shirt, mostly unbuttoned and rolled at the elbow, dark blue pants with a red stripe going down the outside of each leg, and shiny black shoes—a half-dressed marine.

Her mouth fell a little. She'd never seen him in uniform, and even this partial peek made her breath catch.

"Carrie." His hair was slicked back, shimmery in the light as if it were wet and making her long to touch it. He came around the front of her truck and she kept the door between them, not consciously, though when she realized it, she let it slide. The more separation the better. It would be too easy to find herself in those arms.

"I'm on my way out."

"Give me five minutes. That's all I have before Cole hunts me down. I had to slip out when his back was turned."

She smiled reluctantly, imaging the older Haywoods trying to keep Levi in line. "You'd better get back. It's almost time for the wedding."

"I don't care." He moved around the door, his gaze hot and intense, and reached for her. "Please don't go."

"Levi, don't."

"I won't beg. I might want to, but I won't."

"I'm not asking you to—"

"Damn it, Carrie. You're all I think about. Let me show you that we can make this work." He held an envelope out to her, and though she itched to take it, she didn't. Hope was false. Hadn't that been proven the other day? Going back to her safe little cocoon in Wyoming was better for everyone.

"It can't."

He grimaced, frustration etched in the lines by his eyes. "You want me to tell you that it's too hard? That you're not worth it, Carrie? Is that what you want me to say? Because those words will never come out of my mouth." He caught her wrist and with one tug, brought her up against his chest. Despair spread to near-panic level. She had to leave. Now. "Please don't tell me I'm losing you. Damn it, I let you go once. I won't do it again."

The need to hold him was suffocating. Finding strength, Carrie backed up and freed herself from his grip "You don't have to, Levi. I'm letting *you* go."

His chest rose and fell rapidly, the shirt dipping into the muscles of his abdomen, teasing her. The purity of his honor, of his character and the deeply rooted way he wanted to care for her, teased her more. What kind of idiot let go of a love like that?

With a little shake of his head, Levi stepped back and looked at the ground. She did, too, noticing that a smudge of dirt had dulled the sheen of his shoe tips; a fine layer of dust settled over the hem of his perfectly pressed pants.

Spinning on her heel, she walked toward the house, feeling his gaze on her, forcing her body to obey. She hadn't even made it to the porch when she heard his truck back up, turn and pull away. Covering her mouth with a palm, Carrie stood there for long minutes until the quakes going through her body stopped enough that she could walk back to the truck.

It was done.

The rain was so heavy Carrie could barely see out the windshield. She'd just made it past Greenbrook when the storm started to trickle in. Forty-five minutes later and it was pouring and interfering with her ability to safely see the road. Frustrated and pissed off, she was forced to pull into a small town just off the highway. Finding a café, she parked and sat in the truck for a while, not really in the mood to be in public, but not wanting to be cooped up in her vehicle, either.

She wanted Montana behind her and these past ten days as far away as possible. Each mile had brought Levi's image to mind, how he looked in that half-dressed uniform, the sincerity and hurt on his face. Why did she have to love him so much?

The plop of rain on the cab roof reminded her of spending the night on his couch, wrapped in his arms and inhaling his scent of whiskey, aftershave, and sexy man. With a groan, Carrie hit the steering wheel with her palm. She wasn't one to feel sorry for herself, but damn it, her medical bullshit had robbed so much from her life. Always on the fringe of independence, having to rely on others just in case.

Why couldn't she just have the life she wanted? Carrie glanced in the rearview mirror. She almost didn't recognize herself—her eyes dull, mascara smeared from the crying stint she'd had on the way. The hard line of her mouth didn't quite prevent her lower lip from trembling, or the ache in her throat from going away.

She wiped at her smeared eyeliner, then rummaged around on the passenger seat for her wallet. She had a pile of stuff tossed there, a sweater and a blanket, water bottle, an extra bag of insulin. Reaching under the sweater, she touched paper that she didn't recall putting there. A manila envelope. Carrie pulled it out from beneath the pile, the neatly scrawled handwriting dark against the paper.

I'll never stop waiting for you.

Oh, God. It was the envelope Levi had tried to give her earlier. He must have tossed it inside when she'd gone up to the house. Clutching it to her chest, she put her wallet and keys in her pocket and dashed from the truck to the café. It was nearly empty, a lone waitress making her rounds of the few occupied tables. Taking a seat by the window, Carrie lay the envelope down with shaking hands.

"Wet enough for ya?"

No, no, no small talk. She didn't have the patience for it right now, not when she was tied up in knots. Carrie smiled at the waitress and made a noncommittal sound. "Diet Coke, please," she said. "And, I don't know… Pie?" Something with sugar in it. She was being a rebel because feelings. At least she wouldn't have to worry about her blood sugar taking a dive with a big slice of pie in her belly.

"Cherry, apple—"

"Cherry. Thanks."

Alone again, she flipped over the envelope, finding no outward indication of what was inside. She put it right side up again, running her finger back and forth over Levi's handwriting. The vent at her feet kicked on and blew hot air up her legs. Shrugging out of her sweater, she stared at the packet as if she could see straight through it. Chiding herself for being stubborn, she opened the top and pulled out the contents.

Three sheets of paper, the first glossy with a picture of a golden retriever puppy being held in mysterious arms. The dog wore a red collar with a heart logo on it with the outline of a dog's face embroidered inside. She scanned the page, finding handwriting beneath the image that looked suspiciously like Levi's as well.

This is Bo. In six months, he'll be a certified diabetic assist dog. He's specially trained to recognize impending low blood sugar by the smell of your breath, and warn you that you need to take some sugar.

She flipped to the next page where another image of Bo, playfully lying in the grass with an orange vest on, came into view.

Bo has been reserved for you.

The last page had pictures of a therapy center not unlike the one Levi proposed for Agate Falls. Mind spinning, she looked closer, realizing it was the main center in California that wanted to open in Montana. The description below stated they weren't just a therapeutic riding center, but also a training center for medical assist dogs. On the side of the page, two printed tickets were stapled. She pulled them off.

Airline tickets, flying into LAX.

If you're willing, Bo and his trainers would like to meet you so they can show you what's possible. And if the time comes to find a way through the darkness, we will. Start a new life with me, Sunshine.

Another line was scribbled underneath, as if he'd added it last minute…maybe right before he'd thrown the envelope in the truck.

Come home, Carrie Lynn.

"Gurrrl!" The waitress's voice startled Carrie into dropping the papers. "I don't know who that boy is, but *I* want to go home to him." She set down the pie and soda with a sheepish grin. "Sorry, couldn't help but see."

Speechless, Carrie just shook her head and carefully gathered up the papers. The waitress sat across from her, arms folded, big golden earrings swinging. "What are you going to do?"

"I'm… I'm…"

She'd never heard of a diabetic assist dog, but somehow Levi had. Possibilities. Hadn't he said they'd find the possibilities? Fear had always been her biggest obstacle between what was and the possibility of what could be. Levi in his uniform this morning was a reminder that chances were meant to be taken and opportunities grabbed. If he hadn't done those things for himself, he'd still be lying in a hospital bed, existing instead of living.

The waitress leaned closer, eyes wide and lips parted in anticipation. "What? What are you going to do?"

Carrie hugged the papers to her chest and looked out the window, watched water droplets slide down the glass. "I'm going to wait out the rain."

Chapter Twenty-Three

Levi hated that he wanted this wedding over with, but he wanted this wedding over with. The sooner he could shed his military dress uniform, the better. He was antsy as hell, could barely keep his mind on anything except Carrie. As soon as this was over, he was heading to Wyoming.

He'd resolved to take the high road, to make his gesture and sit back and wait. Yeah, that had lasted less than four hours. There'd be no more damn waiting. Thanks to the weather, the wedding had been seriously delayed as the outdoor seating and decorations had been moved to the indoor arena. The guests had been well supplied with whiskey and drinks to tide them over, and by the time Maeve and Jim finally exchanged vows two hours late, no one seemed to mind having to wait.

And now the thing had turned into one big party inside the arena, and no matter how many times he tried to weasel his way outside, Levi kept getting detained. He was ready to punch someone if it meant getting the hell out of this crowd. Excusing himself as politely as he could from a conversation he'd gotten tangled up in, Levi pulled at the collar of his uniform and started to weave his way through the partygoers.

"Uncle Levi!" He stopped short at the sweet voice, looking down to see Birdie running toward him with a chicken under one arm. The skirt of his niece's white flower-girl dress was dragging over the sand floor, kicking up a little tornado behind her. "Look, it's Fred Bologna!" She thrust the rusty red bird at him. On impulse, he took the chicken in both hands and held it away from him. The poor thing had ribbons tied around its neck—Birdie's hair ribbons, apparently. "And Puff!" She produced a snow-white kitten from under her other arm, wearing a silver-and-blue garter as a collar.

"Um, Birdie, where did you get this?" He streaked a finger over the garter with the sudden image of the little girl stripping it off Grandma's leg. Frowning, he shook off the image.

"Grandma said, 'What the heck do I need to wear this thing for?' and gave it to me." With that, she turned the way she'd come and darted off with the cat, leaving Levi to spin around after her, holding the chicken at arm's length and calling after her.

And looking up to see Carrie.

Her mouth fell open at the same time his lips went numb. The slow sweep of her eyes plunged his body into a type of awakening that was slow to reach his brain.

"I have a chicken," he said. She smiled.

"You, and your chicken, look amazing."

Catching the elbow of the first guy who passed him, Levi pawned off the bird, ignoring the man's protest, before taking Carrie's arm and leading her away. They didn't get far before the way was blocked by partygoers.

"Carrie—"

"You got me a dog." He took in her messy hair and

wrinkled jeans, old sweater. It seemed much longer than a few hours ago that he'd seen her.

"Yes."

Someone bumped into her, driving Carrie forward. Levi caught her with one hand, afraid to embrace her. She was tense and he didn't want to hope, to push. Her hand slid up his arm, gripping the fabric lightly, yet with a desperate edge that seemed like she was hanging on. He cupped her elbow, steadying her and himself.

"I don't want to be scared. I want to live my life." The words rushed out of her, urgent but with an excited edge.

Hope broke free and welled up in him. They'd waited so long for this chance. "I want that, too."

"I'm going to be a lot of work, Levi."

He pulled her in and her arms went around him, his hands finding her hair and holding her tightly. "Never too much for me."

"I'm going to have bad days."

"I still have them. We'll have them together."

She pulled back, grabbed him by the middle of the collar, and pulled him down. "Then yes," she whispered against his lips. A commotion behind him made them turn to see. Cole leading a wobbling Rylan by the elbow as she cupped her pregnant belly with both hands. His brother's eyes were wide, shocked even, his steps urgently pulling Rylan along. With a disbelieving look, Cole passed Levi with an exuberant, "Her water broke!"

"Cole, slow down! You're going too fast for her to keep up!" Sophie rushed by next, waving a hand at her brother-in-law, who showed no interest in listening.

"She'd better wait until we get to the hospital to have that baby," Tucker grumbled as he hurried after his wife. "I do not want to see that mess."

Sophie tossed her two-toned brown and blond hair as she

looked over her shoulder at her husband. "Well, get prepared big boy, 'cause this will be you and me in January." Carrie and Levi shared a look, Carrie bursting into a smile when Tucker stumbled, nearly falling to one knee.

"Wait. What?" His voice trailed off as the crowd swallowed the group. Glad to have the attention off them, Levi tipped Carrie's chin and kissed her softly, sweet and slow. Pausing to take a breath, he whispered, "Yes, you will what?"

She paused about long enough to give him a heart attack, her arms slipping around his neck. "Yes, Levi. I'll stay."

Epilogue

Weston Cole Haywood looked pretty cute snuggled in his uncle Levi's arms, if Carrie said so herself. Birdie only added to the cuteness factor by reaching up to fuss over her six-month-old baby brother and beg Levi to hand him over. Without missing a beat, Carrie tapped Birdie on the shoulder and handed her the leash for one wiggling Bo, who was more than happy to kiss the little girl's face until she fell on the ground in a fit of giggles.

Around them, Maeve and Jim, Sophie with her beautiful pregnant belly, holding Tucker's hand, and friends and family had gathered for the groundbreaking of the therapeutic riding center, which would be built right there at Agate Falls and welcome therapists and clients in the spring. Funding had been secured, the plans finalized—which included the sunflower stained glass panel she'd found and repaired being inset into the front door. Levi was the primary investor and manager. He'd been splitting his time between the ranches, though each week seemed to find him at Agate Falls more, where they'd settled in. Carrie wasn't complaining.

Though they'd sold off more stock to help balance the books, the cash Levi had invested in the place, plus his management help, was turning things around. Taking a place at Levi's side, Carrie reached for the baby and simply watched as Cole said a few words about the therapy center to the crowd. This was good. It was all amazingly good. She was secure, surrounded by love, and the inevitability of her changing sight wasn't as terrifying as it was before.

Levi had made sure of that. Pushy, stubborn man that he was. She looped her arm through his and tipped her chin up for his kiss. She'd never had a chance against him in the first place.

No woman in her right mind could resist a cowboy.

About the Author

Elizabeth Otto grew up in a Wisconsin town the size of a postage stamp, where riding your horse to the grocery store, and skinny dipping after school were perfectly acceptable. No surprise that she writes about small communities and country boys. She's the author of paranormal, and hot, emotional, contemporary romance, and has no guilt over frequently making her readers cry. When not writing, she works full-time as an Emergency Medical Technician for a rural ambulance service. Elizabeth lives with her very own country boy and their three children in, shockingly, a small Midwestern town.

Discover more romance from Entangled...

THE PLAYER'S GAME
a Player's Pact novel by Alice Gaines

NFL quarterback Grant Howard has it all—money, fame... and women. Lots of women. But he'd trade it all in for another chance with his ex-wife, Katy. Then, at a wedding, he runs into her, and the sparks are still there. Could this be a second chance for them? He hopes so. At least, until Katy tells him what she really wants.

REFORMING THE CEO
a South Beach novel by Marisa Cleveland

Reece Rowe's going to get a taste of what she's been missing and heads to hot Vincent Ferguson's office to find out what the women in South Beach already seem to know about him. CEO Vin Ferguson has to improve his image with his financial backers, and his friends suggest dating a respectable woman. Ridiculous. Because delectable but snooty socialites like Reece are out of his league. But he can't believe what she just proposed...

NO PLAYER REQUIRED
a Biggest Little Love Story novel by JoAnn Sky

Billionaire casino magnate Rafael "Rafa" Salord is forced to exchange caviar for cowboy boots when he's sent to "grow up" and run his father's newly acquired casino in the middle of nowhere downtown Reno. When he crosses paths with feisty Destiny Morson, he starts to wonder if that nonsense about love-at-first-sight might actually be true. Maybe it's time to trade in his playboy status and bet on something more.

www.ingramcontent.com/pod-product-compliance
Lightning Source LLC
Chambersburg PA
CBHW060940180626
46817CB00004B/1635